AT THE FRENCH BARON'S BIDDING

BY

FIONA HOOD-STEWART

MILLS & BOON®

First published in Great Britain 2005
Large Print edition 2006
Harlequin Mills & Boon Limited,
Eton House, 18-24 Paradise Road,
Richmond, Surrey TW9 1SR

© Fiona Hood-Stewart 2005

ISBN 0 263 18926 0

Set in Times Roman 16½ on 18 pt.
16-0106-50881

Printed and bound in Great Britain
by Antony Rowe Ltd, Chippenham, Wiltshire

AT THE FRENCH
BARON'S BIDDING

CHAPTER ONE

IT WASN'T that she didn't want to go back to France, for in truth she did. But as the chauffeur-driven car drove sedately through the gates of the Manoir that she remembered only vaguely from early childhood, Natasha de Saugure experienced a rush of mixed emotions: she really should have responded to her grandmother's summons sooner.

Yet the past hung between them, and had impeded her from doing so. Now, Natasha hoped that it wouldn't be too late. Her grandmother had sounded so frail over the phone. But taking leave from her job with a humanitarian organisation in Africa wasn't easy. She had, in the short space of time she'd been employed, acquired a post of much responsibility. She owed it to the starving mothers and children they were so desperately trying to save to be there.

Still, after the car had crunched across the gravel driveway and come to a stop, Natasha stepped out and breathed a unique fragrance that she recognized as fresh lavender and thyme; she knew she'd been right to come.

'*Voilà, mademoiselle.*' The driver smiled at her over his shoulder before jumping out and solicitously opening the car door.

'*Merci.*' Natasha smiled back. In a quick movement she straightened her long ash-blonde hair and glanced up at the ancient stone façade of the Manoir: its rounded turrets at each corner, the lead-tiled roof, the ivy that weaved over its centuries-old stone walls. Making her way towards the stately front door past grand stone pots filled with well-trimmed shrubs, Natasha sighed. It was many years since she'd last seen her grandmother—after the irreparable rift between the old lady and Natasha's father when he'd married out of his set.

All at once the ancient front door creaked, opened, and an old, white-haired man in uniform appeared on the steps.

'*Bienvenue, mademoiselle,*' he said, his face breaking into a wrinkled smile. '*Madame* will be so pleased.'

'*Bonjour*, Henri,' she said; she'd heard her mother talk about the old retainer. She stepped inside the flagstoned hall and gazed about her at the high ceilings and doorways leading this way and that into the warren of passages and rooms beyond. Little by little vague memories unfurled as long-forgotten images jumped forth to greet her.

But the question that still tugged at her as she entered the Manoir was why, after all these years of silence, had her grandmother insisted she come? There had been little in the letter she'd received to indicate her reasons; little in her imperative tone on the phone to suggest she'd unbent after all this time.

Yet insist she had.

And, despite her first inclination to refuse, Natasha had known she had to come. After all, notwithstanding the past, now that both her parents were dead Natasha was the old lady's only living relative.

After Henri had exclaimed, with a tear in his eye, at seeing her again, all grown up, thrilled that she'd remembered his name, Natasha followed him up the stone staircase, amazed at how much she recognized. Over twenty years had elapsed since her last visit to Normandy, but so much felt familiar: the scents, the light pouring through the tall windows and bathing the muted walls, the echo of her heels resonating on the well-trodden steps. And something else that she couldn't quite identify.

'*Madame* is waiting for you upstairs in the small salon,' Henri pronounced in stentorian tones.

'Then I had better go to her at once.' Natasha smiled again, her green eyes sparkling with amusement. The situation was so dreadfully formal, as though she'd walked into another time and place.

With a small bow the butler led the way slowly up the wide staircase. Natasha realized that he suffered from arthritis and found the climb difficult. She was about to suggest that he simply tell her where the salon was and she would find it herself when she realized that would be a grave breach of etiquette. Henri, who had worked here all his life, would not take kindly to any deviation from the rigorous habits her grandmother kept.

Soon they stopped before a white and gold door. Henri knocked, then gently opened it. 'She awaits you,' he pronounced in a hushed tone.

Natasha swallowed. Suddenly this didn't seem quite as simple as she'd imagined it would when she was back in Khartoum. She was a compassionate person by nature, but the drastic way her grandmother had cut her own son out of her life had made Natasha distrustful of the older woman, whom she barely recalled.

Then, knowing she must get on with it, Natasha gathered up her courage and stepped through the door that Henri was holding open and into the high-ceilinged, shaded room. It took a moment or two for her eyes to adjust to the half-light. Then she gazed over at the tiny white-haired figure shrouded under a silk coverlet on an antique pink-velvet day-bed under the window.

'Ah, *mon enfant*, finally you have arrived.'

The voice was a thin whisper and, despite her initial instinctive desire to hold back, Natasha's natural empathy asserted itself. Instead of the grandmother who'd rejected her and her family for most of her life, she saw instead a feeble old lady in need of help. Quickly she approached.

'Yes, Grandmère. I am here.'

'At last.' The old lady turned her once beautiful, fine-boned features towards Natasha, the pale blue eyes searching. 'Come here, child, and sit next to me. I have waited so long for you to come.'

'I know. But I couldn't get away before. We have a humanitarian crisis on our hands right now,' she explained, perching her tall, slim figure gingerly on the edge of a spindly gilded chair.

'Never mind. The main thing is that you are here now. Henri.' The querulous voice had not lost its authoritarian tone. *'Le thé, s'il-vous-plaît.'*

'Tout de suite, madame.'

With another little bow Henri retired, closing the door behind him.

'Are you sure he can manage?' Natasha asked, glancing doubtfully at the closed door.

'Manage? Of course Henri can manage,' the old lady responded peremptorily, straightening herself against the cushions with determination. 'He has been managing since before the war, when he came here as assistant *aide de cuisine*. But enough of that.' The old lady waved a delicate white bejewelled hand. 'Tell me about yourself, child. It has been too long. Far too long.' She let out a tremulous sigh. 'I am to blame for that, I know. But it is too late for regrets.' Her eyes rested on Natasha as though assessing her. Even though she was physically fragile, there was nothing weak about the old lady. Clearly she had all her faculties about her.

'Well, there's nothing much to tell. When I finished school I went to university. But when my parents died three years ago in the car crash, I just wanted to get away as far as I could, so I dropped out. That's when the job in Africa came up.' She shrugged, bit her lip. 'It seemed the right thing to do.'

'And are you happy in your work?' Her grandmother eyed her piercingly.

'Yes. I am. It's very exhausting, and emotionally harrowing, but it's also terribly rewarding.'

The old lady nodded. 'You are a good and compassionate person. Unlike me,' she added with a bitter laugh. 'I was always more concerned about my own well-being than that of others. Now I've paid the price for my selfish behaviour.' She let out another long sigh and closed her eyes.

Natasha hesitated. Part of her was still reticent, remembering her father's sorrow and her mother's sense of guilt at having estranged the man she loved from his family. There was no denying that it was hard to shove a lifetime's grievances under the carpet and pretend that all was well. Still, she didn't want the past to affect the future.

'Grandmère, we all make mistakes in life.'

'That we do.' The old lady nodded. 'I wonder, is it possible for you to forgive me for all the harm I have done to your family, Natasha? I wish so deeply now that I had been more enlightened, that I had not estranged my dearest Hubert as I did.'

Natasha hesitated, saw the flicker of hope in the elderly woman's eyes, and her heart went out to her. 'Of course, Grandmère. Let's look towards the future, and not into the past.'

'Ah.' The old lady rested her hand on Natasha's and smiled a frail yet gentle smile.

'I was right to have you come. Very right indeed.' She laid her fingers over Natasha's and two women sat thus for several minutes, a new bond forming between them.

Then a knock at the door announced Henri with the tea, and the spell was broken. Natasha jumped up to open the door while her grandmother issued imperative orders regarding the placement of the tea tray. She might be old, Natasha realized, a smile hovering, but she had all her wits about her and her authority still stood strong.

An hour later they had sipped tea, exchanged stories, and the old lady was obviously very tired.

'I'll leave you and unpack,' Natasha said, rising.

'Yes, *mon enfant*. That is a good idea. I'm afraid I won't join you for dinner, but Henri will see to you. Come and say goodnight, won't you?'

'Very well.' Natasha bent down and dropped a light kiss on her grandmother's withered cheek. 'I'll see you later.'

'Yes, my child. I shall be waiting.'

*   *   *

After undoing her case and placing her clothes inside the beautiful lavender-scented armoire in the faded yet elegant blue satin-draped bedroom she had been allotted, Natasha moved to the window and gazed out over the lush green countryside. In the distance she could see a medieval castle, its ramparts etched against the translucent sky. Shading her eyes, she distinguished a pennant flying from the turret. She thought of William the Conqueror, of the Norman invasion. Perhaps it was a historical monument that she could visit.

It was late spring. Flowers bloomed as though they'd constantly burst forth from one day to the next, their rich hues framing a weathered stone fountain; flowerbeds dotted with lupins and roses surrounded the velvet-smooth lawn. It was peaceful and lovely, as though caught in a time warp. Natasha glanced at her watch and wondered if she'd have time for a wander before dinner.

Deciding that she did, she slipped on a pair of sneakers and went downstairs. There was no one in the hall so she stepped out of the front door and began walking, tilting her face up towards the fast-moving cloud, enjoying the wind mussing her hair.

Soon she had wandered well beyond the lawn and the garden perimeter, and was walking across a field, enjoying the fresh breeze and the exercise. Suddenly she heard the sound of hooves. Stopping abruptly, she turned to find out who it might be, surprised to see a tall dark man in jeans and riding boots astride a nervous chestnut horse. The stranger reined in abruptly. He did not, Natasha realized, somewhat taken aback, look too pleased.

'Who are you?' he threw at her in French, in the tone of one unused to being thwarted.

Natasha glanced up at him, stiffening. 'I don't see what it has to do with you who I am,' she retorted in fluent French.

'It has everything to do with me as I am the owner of this land.'

'Well, if you are, I'm sorry I trespassed. I had no ill intention,' she replied in a haughty tone, damned if she was going to be ordered about by this obnoxious man.

'Very well,' he snapped. 'See that it doesn't happen again.'

On that peremptory note he swung the horse around and galloped off, leaving Natasha fuming, her fists balled in anger.

The nerve of the man. Why, he was the rudest creature she'd ever encountered.

It was later than she'd thought and deciding that if she really had stepped onto someone else's land she'd better make her way back to the Manoir, she walked fast. As she approached the stately building she stopped and gazed at it, bathed now in the glow of the setting sun, copper drainpipes glinting on the roof. Natasha drank in the sight, determined to banish the image of the dark and odious horseman. Still, as she entered the hall and made her way quickly up to her room, she couldn't help wondering who the ignominious rider could be.

Obviously a neighbour if he owned the land. Come to think of it, if he'd had a pleasanter expression she might even have thought him good-looking, she conceded, remembering the dark scowling features and the black hair swept back from his autocratic brow. Not that it was any of her business, she reminded herself. Still, she'd ask her grandmother who he was.

At eight o'clock sharp Natasha, dressed in a dark blue silk dress she thought her grandmother would approve of, glided gracefully down the main stairway and was met by Henri, who immediately guided her into the formal dinning room. Natasha sighed. She had no desire to sit alone at a table big enough to seat sixteen. But she said nothing. This was the way things were—she'd heard it often enough from her father's stories about his boyhood. There was little use saying she'd rather have a tray in the sitting room, as it wasn't going to happen.

After the meal she got up, relieved to have finished, and made her way upstairs to her grandmother's bedroom. She'd say goodnight before it was too late, then go to her room, have a bath in the huge antique tub, and curl up in the blue satin-swathed four-poster and read.

After three unanswered knocks she decided to open the door and peer inside. She smiled when she saw the old lady sleeping. Perhaps she shouldn't disturb her. Yet something pushed her to stay, and she moved towards the bed and gazed down at her grandmother. The Comtesse de Saugure lay perfectly still, her expression peaceful. Then all at once Natasha gasped, leaned forward, and felt for the older woman's pulse.

But there was none.

Heart trembling, Natasha tried to wake her.

'Grandmère,' she murmured, gently touching her shoulder. 'Please wake up.' But she met with only silence. Horrified, her hands shaking, Natasha stood straighter and allowed the truth to sink in.

Her grandmother was dead.

CHAPTER TWO

THE early Norman chapel was filled with mourners, both local and foreign. Old retainers who had worked for the Comtesse for most of their lives lined the narrow road as the hearse made its way through the countryside. Natasha followed in the ancient Rolls, driven by Henri.

Now, as she stood alone in the front pew, dressed in black, listening to the priest read the funeral service, Natasha felt both sad and bewildered. She knew no one except for Henri and his wife Mathilde, standing respectfully in the pew behind her. Part of her shock was caused by the meeting she'd had this morning with the local notary who'd come to read her grandmother's will. To her astonishment Natasha had learned that she was her grandmother's sole beneficiary. She had inherited not only the château in Normandy, but the Comtesse's sumptuous flat in the *16ième arrondissement* in Paris, and her villa on the Côte d'Azur.

Natasha had gathered her thoughts and prepared to follow the coffin down the aisle when all at once she looked up and saw the man she'd encountered in the field, seated in the opposite pew. He looked different dressed in a dark suit and tie, with his hair groomed. Their eyes met and once more Natasha wondered who he was.

Then, turning away, she followed the pallbearers out of the church to the graveyard where the Comtesse would end her life's journey, laid to rest among the ancient crooked headstones, many of which bore the name of Saugure upon them. As the coffin was lowered into the earth and the priest spoke the words she'd heard not that long ago when her parents were buried, Natasha experienced a moment of deep sadness and solitude.

Now she had no one left. Not even the estranged grandmother whom she'd hoped to get to know. Now she had only herself to count on.

Raoul d'Argentan stood a few steps away from the mourners, eyes fixed on the young woman standing next to the grave. Who was this granddaughter of the Comtesse de Saugure who had appeared out of nowhere on the day of her death? He knew, of course, that Marie Louise de Saugure had been estranged from her only son. But that all went back a long way. This, he supposed, must be his daughter. But what a strange coincidence that she should have returned only for her grandmother to die. Well, it was none of his business. The Saugures and the Argentans had been neighbours for several centuries and knew each other well. But their history had not always been pleasant. There were instances dating back a few hundred years, grievances that still rankled. Not that he cared. He had his own affairs to contend with: his auction house in Paris, which dealt in some of Europe's finest art, and, of course, the estate to run.

As he walked back to his car Raoul supposed that he should pay his respects before his departure for Paris the next morning. It was only polite, after all, to offer his condolences. Though it seemed cynical when the girl obviously barely knew the woman who had left her a fortune.

As he drove off down the hill Raoul cast a quick glance in the rearview mirror. The mourners were leaving the graveyard and he glimpsed the woman once more. Whatever else she was, she was damn lovely, that was for sure.

Telling himself to stop being ridiculous— the last thing he needed was to find himself attracted to a Saugure—he pressed his foot on the accelerator and made his way back to his estate, determined not to think about the lovely wan face and that pair of limpid green eyes, which, despite every instinct, he'd felt strangely attracted to. He consoled himself with the fact that she was unattractively dressed, had no chic at all. In fact, he would go as far as saying she looked frumpy. With a shake of his head he headed back to his château and thought about the upcoming telephone call to New York that he needed to make.

'Mademoiselle?'

'Yes, Henri?' Natasha looked up from the desk where she was going through some of her grandmother's papers and smiled.

'The Baron d'Argentan is here to offer his condolences.'

'Right.' She sighed, laying down the missive. Rising, she straightened her one black dress, realizing she simply must go into Deauville and acquire some suitable clothes. This was not the first neighbour come to pay their respects and satisfy their curiosity regarding the new owner of the Manoir, and she needed to dress accordingly. Better get used to it, she realized, following Henri across the hall to the formal drawing room where the butler liked to install the guests.

But, on stepping inside the room, Natasha felt her pulse leap when she recognized the tall figure silhouetted against the window. She was about to speak, then stopped, and swallowed.

'I come to present my condolences,' he said, in a haughty, rich baritone that seemed to resonate through the elegant room. Then he stepped forward and, raising Natasha's fingers to his lips, bent his head towards them.

'Thank you,' she murmured, feeling her pulse pick up speed. His fingers felt strangely vibrant, as though an electric current were coursing through them. 'Uh, do sit down,' she said hurriedly, taking a step back and indicating the Louis Quinze chair opposite.

'Thank you.' He waited for her to sit, then followed suit. Natasha was relieved when the door opened and Henri entered with a bottle of champagne, which he proceeded to open.

'I have not had the pleasure of your acquaintance,' the Baron remarked, placing one leg over the other. 'I wasn't aware that the Comtesse had a granddaughter.' He raised a quizzical black brow at her, as though questioning her authenticity. 'I don't seem to recall meeting you in the past.'

Natasha bristled and felt her cheeks flush, a flash of anger take hold. 'That is because I haven't been here for many years,' she said coldly.

'Aha. That would explain it.'

'Yes.'

Natasha felt irritated with herself. Why was she allowing this stranger to make her feel ill at ease? She was, after all, in her own house now, for whatever that was worth.

They each accepted a glass of champagne from Henri and the Baron raised his. 'To a very great lady. The Comtesse will be sorely missed in the region—won't she, Henri?' he said, addressing the butler.

'Ah, *oui*, Monsieur le Baron, she most certainly will.' Henri nodded in agreement. 'But of course we are blessed to have *mademoiselle*,' he added quickly.

'Very true. This has come as rather a surprise to the community.' The Baron twiddled his flute and studied her lazily.

'I hope not an unwelcome one?' Natasha retorted, her chin tilting upwards, anger at his high-handed manners and the idle way his eyes coursed over her increasing by the moment.

'Unwelcome? Not at all. In fact, quite the opposite. You will be a breath of fresh air. That is if you plan to stay here?' Again the brow flew up. It was as though he were searching for something amiss, something untoward.

'It is far too soon for me to decide what to do. I haven't made up my mind yet,' she responded, hoping her tone would dampen any other questions. Yet part of her wanted him to believe her, resented that he should find anything suspicious about her. For it was true. She hadn't decided what to do with her new inheritance. Part of her wanted to run back to

Africa, to the safety of her job. Yet another part, a part she hadn't known existed before, was struck by a new sense of loyalty to her lineage and the duties that came with the inheritance. It was her grandmother's personal letter to her that had struck a chord. *You are the only Saugure left to continue the line...* Incredibly, the old lady had expected her to assume all her responsibilities.

The Baron stayed for several more minutes, making polite small talk, then rose. 'If there is anything I can help you with, Henri has my numbers. As you've probably gathered,' he said, a sudden wicked smile curving his well-defined lips, 'I am your neighbour.'

'That much became pretty obvious the other day,' she muttered dryly, smiling despite her initial desire to dislike him.

'Yes, well, I'm sorry for the way I greeted you that day. It was rude and bad-mannered. I'm hoping that, to make up for it, you might come and dine with me one day. Perhaps I can bring you up to speed on the area.' He took her hand and squeezed it in his, holding it slightly longer than necessary, and again

Natasha experienced that same pulsating tingle.

'That would be very nice,' she accepted, surprising herself as she extricated her fingers from his.

'Good. Then I'll expect you tomorrow.' He gave a satisfied nod.

'I—I haven't got my schedule here,' she mumbled.

'Oh? Your timetable is already very booked up?' He smiled down at her, his dark eyes brimming with mirth.

Natasha blushed once more. 'That's not what I meant.'

'Then in that case I'll expect you at eight tomorrow evening. Henri will drive you.' With a quick nod he turned on his heel and left the room.

'Well,' Natasha exclaimed under her breath as she walked to the window and let out a long huff. The man certainly didn't lack nerve. Why, he was impossibly authoritarian. And, since she hadn't refused, she was now stuck with having dinner with him. Which reminded her of her desperate need to buy some clothes. Not that it mattered what she looked like, she qualified hastily; he was just a neighbour, and quite a rude one at that. But still, for some inexplicable reason she wanted to look her best. Perhaps it was part of her new-found duty to her name. After all, she must keep up the family reputation.

What on earth had caused him to invite this dowdy-looking Englishwoman to dinner when he'd had every intention of leaving for Paris immediately? Raoul wondered as he drove down the driveway and out onto the country road beyond. It was nonsensical and stupid to delay his return to town. Particularly to dine with someone as un-chic as his new neighbour. The woman's hair looked as if it hadn't seen a hairdresser in years, and her clothes didn't bear mentioning!

Perhaps, he concluded, shaking his head as he entered the castle gates, it was because he didn't want to go back to Paris, where he would have to deal with another of Clothilde's jealous rages.

Slowing the car to a halt in front of his massive oak front door, Raoul glanced at his mobile. Just as he'd thought, there were several missed calls from her. He rolled his eyes and huffed, passing a hand thoughtfully over his bronzed chin. He really must bring this relationship to an end. Apparently staying away for longer periods of time than he usually did wasn't doing the trick. Raoul sighed and alighted from the car. Like most men, he hated facing disagreeable situations. And Clothilde was certainly that, with her hysterical scenes and childish moods. Why, he wondered, had he got involved with her in the first place?

Stepping into the morning breeze, Raoul watched as the stable boys led two of his favourite horses across the cobblestoned yard, then stood for a moment on the edge of the well, dropping a pebble inside. Why not admit to himself that he'd succumbed to Clothilde's charm for the same reason he had all the others: because it was easier to date top models who shimmied in and out of his life than commit to anything more serious. At thirty-six he was a confirmed bachelor, and had no intention of changing his single status. Much to the disappointment of several mothers of suitable candidates to become the future Baroness d'Argentan.

His mouth took on a cynical twist. Women were ambitious gold-diggers, as he'd found out to his cost several years earlier. He would not repeat the mistake of falling for one again. And, speaking of gold-diggers, he reflected, making his way towards the medieval castle that had been in his family for centuries, perhaps Natasha de Saugure was yet another one. After all, this sudden arrival of hers was too damned coincidental to be mere fluke. He just hoped she hadn't frightened her grandmother into having a heart attack.

But as he walked through the great hall Raoul realized with a smile that this was probably a foolish thought. He had known Marie Louise de Saugure since he was a child. If anyone had done the terrifying it could have been her. Still, he felt wary of Natasha. As he would be of any Saugure. Which was obviously why he'd felt the need to ask her to dine: to delve deeper into her motives for coming here in the first place. The more he could glean about her, the better; for the past had taught every member of his family to be wary of Saugure women.

And he was no exception.

CHAPTER THREE

NATASHA tilted her head and took another satisfied look at herself in the gilded three-way mirror. It was a long time since she'd bothered about clothes and looking nice. The last few years, tucked away in the African bush with two pairs of jeans and a few faded T-shirts, had not helped her improve her fashion skills. Still, she'd spent time in Deauville that afternoon and taken the advice of a charming shop assistant who, seeing her in doubt, had helped her select a number of items, discarding others with a disparaging wave of her well-manicured hands, saying that beige did not favour *mademoiselle*.

Now, as she looked at her reflection, Natasha had to admit that the woman had been right. Everything she'd chosen—from the pretty pink tweed Chanel suit to the sleek trousers and the attractive cream dress she now wore—spelled chic, smart, and made her look very different from the girl who'd stepped off the plane a few days before. Suddenly she'd been transformed from average to head-turning, thanks to the make-over that Martine, the shop assistant, had insisted on. Upon her excellent advice, Natasha had gone to the top hairdresser in town and had her long hair shaped, washed and blow-dried. The effect, combined with the new outrageously expensive outfit, was staring her right in the face, and she was finding it hard to reconcile the woman in the mirror with who she was inside.

Oh, well, she conceded with a shrug, surely she could get used to improvement? Plus, she was damned if she was going to dine at Raoul d'Argentan's castle looking like something the cat had brought in on a bad day. Which made her wonder uncomfortably, as she turned away from the mirror and stepped into the bathroom to put on some make-up, why he'd asked her over in the first place. Perhaps it was curiosity. After all, everyone must be wondering who she was and why she was here. Although no doubt Monsieur Dubois, the notary, had dropped hints in his various clients' ears. She could imagine just how intriguing it must be for a small community such as this to have her as the new châtelaine.

Which in turn brought her back to the problem of what she was going to do. Was she really prepared to turn her life around one hundred and eighty degrees and come and live in Normandy, away from the world she knew, to pick up a legacy left to her by a woman who'd denied her that same legacy all her life?

Glancing at the ormolu clock on the pink marble mantelpiece, Natasha realized it was getting late and wasn't the moment for soul-searching. She'd think about her life later. Right now she needed to get downstairs, where Henri would be waiting to drive her over to the Baron's.

After a last peek in the mirror, she picked up a smart evening purse and stepped into her new, amazingly comfortable high heels. She took a few tentative steps. Not bad, considering she'd only worn sandals and sneakers for the past three years.

Hoping she wouldn't totter too badly, Natasha made her way to the grand stairway and accomplished her descent without mishap, glad to see Henri waiting for her in the hall.

*   *   *

As the car drew up at the floodlit drawbridge Natasha caught her breath. The Baron's château was amazing. Her grandmother's Manoir was beautiful, but it was also stiff and formal. This place, in contrast, was a maze of twelfth-century turrets, built of heavy stone and obviously impregnable. The men who'd built it were not to be tampered with, was the message it conveyed. All at once she shuddered and wondered about its present owner.

'It is very *impressionnant*, is it not?' Henri said, seeing her gaze up at the ramparts.

'It certainly is. It must be very old.'

'The Argentan family has lived here since before William departed to conquer England,' he relayed proudly. 'The Baron is a descendant of a long line of warriors. They fought many battles and have made many friends and not a few enemies. The first Baron was also named Raoul.'

He drove the car slowly across the drawbridge, which creaked ominously.

'Enemies?' Natasha asked, her brows knitting.

'Yes. There are many tales in the region of the Baron's ancestors, in particular one Regis d'Argentan.'

'Oh?'

'Yes. But I must not go on. All that is in the past and better left buried there. Here we are, *mademoiselle*.' He drew up in the court-yard and quickly stepped out of the car to help her alight before she could ask any further questions.

Minutes later Natasha was being conducted by a wizened butler up an ancient stone stair-way illuminated by torches. Had he put on the full show for her, she wondered, or was there no electricity? The place felt strangely eerie, and an odd sense of *déjà vu* assailed her. But she shrugged it off and, holding her head high as she passed ancient tapestries, braced herself for the evening ahead.

Just as she was wondering where he'd got to, Raoul stepped out of the shadows.

'Good evening,' he said, once more raising her hand to his lips. A curious gleam lit his eyes and he took a step back. 'Excuse me if I seem rude, but I barely recognize you.'

'Is that a compliment?' she asked suspiciously, a laugh hovering.

'I would like to think of it as one,' he confirmed, gallantly steering her into a huge hall with an imposing stone hearth, around which several high-backed velvet chairs were arranged. The fire was burning. Here the lighting seemed at least to be improved. In fact, she realized, it was terribly subtle, with ultra-modern halogens slipped behind the heavy oak beams, pinpointing tapestries and coats of arms which adorned the stone walls.

'Your home is quite amazing,' she said sincerely, aware of his hand at her elbow.

'Thank you, *mademoiselle*—it is *mademoiselle* and not *madame*, I take it?' he enquired smoothly.

'Yes. Of course. I'm not married,' she returned, surprised.

'You object to marriage?'

'It's not something I think about.'

'Really? Well, that is surprising. I thought most women did. How old are you?'

'Twenty-three.'

'Well, that is not a very great age, I admit, but I know a number of girls your age who have several children already.'

'Really?' Natasha tossed her head defiantly. 'I thought women were marrying much later nowadays, and having children in their mid-thirties.'

'Is that what you plan to do?' he asked, that same quizzical brow shooting up, this time with an air of disapproval.

'I have no idea,' she responded tartly. This was not a subject she wished to enlarge upon.

'Ah, so no fiancé dying to drag you to the altar?' he quizzed, motioning to one of the chairs.

'Don't be silly,' she replied with an embarrassed laugh. Thank God he couldn't possibly know about Paul, and all the shame and embarrassment she'd been through at the age of barely nineteen, when he'd dumped her a week before their wedding.

'Very well. Enough about marriage. How about champagne instead?'

'Please.' She sat demurely in the high-backed chair and crossed her legs elegantly. It felt strange to feel so beautifully dressed and feminine, to feel Raoul's eyes devouring her not with the mere curiosity of a neighbour but with patent admiration. And all at once Natasha realized that for the past few years, since her disastrous engagement, she'd been afraid of looking attractive, of facing another relationship, in case she was faced with another misadventure. Well, she was older now, and more mature, she reflected, taking the champagne flute with a smile. She could deal with a little attraction without getting burned or involved.

Raoul settled in the chair opposite. He looked devastatingly handsome tonight, in black pants and a burgundy jacket, his raven hair swept back, his profile caught in the firelight. For an instant Natasha thought he looked just as she would have imagined a Norman Baron must look in his lair.

'So, you are Mademoiselle de Saugure,' he murmured thoughtfully. 'At the risk of sounding nosy, were you expecting to become Marie Louise's heir?'

'Actually, I had no idea. It never occurred to me. I hadn't seen my grandmother in ages. She—she and my father had a falling-out a few years ago,' she finished, not prepared to get into intimate details regarding her family.

'I remember. The Comtesse didn't accept his marriage to your mother. Very foolish, since it made her into a lonely old lady. But understandable.'

'You think so?' Natasha's hackles rose immediately. Her mother's background was something she defended tooth and nail.

'Yes. Your father would have had problems whoever he married. Unless, of course, it had been someone of the Comtesse's own choosing. She was nothing if not authoritative. Liked getting her own way. We had a few tussles ourselves.' He smiled wryly and their eyes met, locking in the candlelight for a few interminable seconds.

'You and my grandmother?'

'Yes. Ever since my parents' demise several years ago I have been Lord of the Manor, so to speak. The Comtesse deemed it her duty to tell me how to run my estate. When I didn't follow her advice to the letter we had a few tiffs. But we got over them and remained fast friends. Strange that you should have arrived so suddenly and that her death should have ensued in such a precipitate manner.'

'If you think it was my fault I can assure you it wasn't,' Natasha replied coolly, hating herself for justifying something she'd had nothing to do with.

'Of course it wasn't. Perhaps she was waiting for you to come before she let go. She's been fairly ill for a while. Did she tell you about the will?'

'No. I only found out when the notary— look, I really don't see what business it is of yours,' she said, suddenly clamming up.

'Pardon,' he said, with a smile that was anything but apologetic. 'You must excuse my curiosity. But you must admit that the circumstances are somewhat unexpected.'

'They are. Which is why I haven't taken any decisions regarding the future, and don't plan to for a while.'

'Very wise.' He nodded, aware that he'd pushed her too far. So the little English girl had fangs under that smooth bland exterior. Interesting. Raoul felt an inner stirring which he immediately recognized as lust. Banishing it at once, aware that a quick hot affair with this woman would hardly be conducive to good neighbourly relations, he rose and extended his hand. 'Let us proceed to dinner,' he said, taking her arm in his. 'I hope you will like what's on the menu.'

'And what is that?' Natasha asked archly. She was finding her feet in this game of light flirtation more easily than she would have believed.

'Oh, *ris de veau*. A speciality my chef loves to prepare.' His eyes sparkled with laughter.

Natasha hesitated, swallowed. 'Isn't that brain?' she asked warily.

'When it is prepared by Alphonse you will not think at all about its origin,' he assured her, leading the way into a vast baronial dining room, where liveried footmen stood behind two chairs at the long table.

'Is everything always so formal?' she asked impulsively as they stood in the entrance. 'I don't think I could live as you do and Grandmère did on an everyday basis. I think it would drive me mad.'

'You prefer a more casual lifestyle?' he asked, looking down at her from his six foot two.

'Yes. I've lived in Africa with refugees in the desert for the past three years. It makes one focus on the essentials in life.'

'I can believe that,' he said as they sat down, and he watched her, intrigued. So she was not some dull little secretary from a provincial backwater but rather a woman who sought adventure in her life. The thought was alluring, gave her an extra aura, and as the candlelight flickered and she unfolded her napkin he took a good look at her face, aware now of just how perfect her features were, and how lithe and attractive her body. Would it be pliant and lithe in bed? he wondered, a sudden image of her lying naked among the sheets causing him to divert his thoughts quickly to avoid any embarrassing consequences.

'Tell me about Africa,' he requested, truly interested in learning more about his intriguing neighbour. Perhaps he'd underestimated her.

Dinner went smoothly. Comfortable talking about a place she was familiar with, a culture which she'd taken the trouble to study, and the humanitarian crisis that she felt so strongly about, Natasha relaxed and became her true self. By the time they'd had coffee and after-dinner drinks, it was close to midnight.

'Gosh, it's getting awfully late. I'd better go home...to the Manoir, I mean. Could I call a taxi?' she enquired, glancing at him across the fireplace.

'Out of the question. I'll drive you.'

'That's very kind, but I don't want to be a nuisance.'

'A beautiful woman is never a nuisance. In fact, *ma chère*, it is a pleasure,' Raoul replied smoothly, executing a small formal bow, his lips curved in a half-smile.

Despite her new desire to be cool and sophisticated, Natasha swallowed. The man was positively devastating when he smiled, she realized, and she was still unused to compliments. To her annoyance the earlier flush returned to her cheeks. Still, letting him drive her home was hardly a big deal.

Once downstairs, they stepped outside into the courtyard and Raoul opened the door of his sleek red Ferrari, clearly amused.

A woman who blushed.

That was an interesting concept—one he hadn't come across in a while. For an instant Clothilde flashed across his mind. He doubted she'd blushed at twelve, let alone now. The thought of the other woman reminded him that tomorrow he would have to go back to Paris and deal with her. For some strange reason it all seemed rather further away than it had earlier in the day, as though his evening with Natasha had somehow obliterated any vestiges of feeling he might have had.

Soon they were driving down dark country lanes before heading into the drive of the Manoir.

'I suppose our families have been neighbours for ever,' Natasha remarked as the wheels crunched the gravel and the vehicle drew up at the front door.

'We have, in effect, been neighbours for going on approximately six hundred years.'

'Who was your ancestor—Regis?' she asked suddenly, remembering Henri's words and turning to try and distinguish his expression in the half-light coming from the outside lamps.

She saw him stiffen. 'Who told you about Regis?' he asked warily.

'Oh, somebody mentioned him. I can't remember who,' she lied, sensing there was more to this story than met the eye. More that she definitely planned to find out.

'Regis was a rather flamboyant character. All families have them, I suppose—a sort of black sheep, in a way. I'll tell you about him some time. It would take too long tonight, *ma chère.*'

'All right.' Natasha pretended not to be intrigued by the story. Someone else could surely tell it. Which made her suddenly determined to become better acquainted with the people on the estate and in the village. Perhaps she could glean some interesting details from them, learn all sorts of things about the past.

Then, when she least expected it, Raoul leaned over and in one smooth, swift movement slipped his hand under her chin and drew her mouth to his.

She should protest, should stop him, should do something, Natasha realized. But it was impossible. For the next thing she knew Raoul's firm lips were parting hers, forcing them to surrender to his will. His arms came about her and her breast cleaved to his hard chest. It was crazy, but all she could do was succumb, allow his probing tongue to wander, seek, explore, and try to ignore the delicious tautness of her nipples, to control the myriad sensations coursing through her body from head to toe. When finally he withdrew his mouth, and stayed staring down at her, she pulled out of his arms, breathless, her pulse racing.

'I'll be back at the end of the week,' he murmured, his voice husky with undisguised desire, 'then we can pick up where we've left off, *ma belle*. I look forward to it already.'

'We will do nothing of the sort,' she retorted, regaining some measure of composure. 'And I'll thank you to leave me alone. I have no need or desire for your attentions. Keep your kisses for your own kind. I have no wish for them.' With that she flung out of the car and, stumbling on the gravel in her high heels, reached the front door.

Henri had given her a heavy key before dinner. Now she inserted it in the lock, her fingers struggling nervously to undo it. 'Oh, bother,' she exclaimed, when it wouldn't turn.

'May I?' Raoul, composed and gentlemanly once more, stepped forward.

'Oh, just go away and leave me alone,' Natasha exclaimed crossly, her nerves still jangling from their unexpected encounter.

'But you'll be stuck out here in the night,' he remarked matter-of-factly. 'Let's be reasonable about this, *ma chère*, after all it was only a kiss.'

With an annoyed huff Natasha stepped back and let Raoul take over. After one expert twist the key turned. *'Voilà,'* he said, smiling down at her with that same mischievous twinkle which had the effect of making her melt inside. *'Bonne nuit*, lovely lady. May you have sweet dreams.' Then he turned abruptly, just as he had the other day. And the next thing she knew he was driving off down the drive as she let herself into the dimly lit hall.

Sleep was impossible. She simply must pull herself together. Instinctively Natasha walked to the library and switched on a lamp. Perhaps another drink would do her good—a nightcap. Or maybe that was the problem. She wasn't used to much alcohol, and, although it hadn't seemed much at the time, over the course of the evening she must have consumed quite a bit. Perhaps a book might do the trick—distract her from the evening's adventure.

But, as she skimmed the packed shelves of classics, Natasha could still feel the touch of Raoul's lips on hers, the tingling sensation that caused her breasts to peak even now, and a strange delicious throbbing travelling through her. It was ridiculous, she reasoned. Outrageous that a man she barely knew could cause such havoc. Why, she hadn't had a boyfriend since Paul, and even then she'd been hesitant to sleep with him, as though something deep down inside had warned her of his future behaviour. But she had. And it hadn't been a success. She'd been afraid, unexcited, but determined to do what she had to. Never in the two years they'd gone out together had she felt anything close to the extreme rush of pleasure she'd derived in those few minutes with Raoul in the car.

'Absurd,' she muttered, glancing at the rows of titles, determined to find something to distract her. All at once her eyes fell upon a large leatherbound volume. *A Concise History of the Famille d'Argentan*, she read. Extracting the large volume from its slot, where it had obviously remained for many years, she brushed off some dust. There was nothing concise about it, she reflected with a grimace, carrying the enormous book over to the sofa.

Wrapping herself in a rug, Natasha opened the stiff cover and began curiously to turn the pages. There was a long detailed family tree. Suddenly her eye fell upon Regis. His dates were interesting. 1768 to 1832. So he had been a young man during the French Revolution. Then, to her amazement, she read a name that was all too familiar: Natasha de Saugure.

The name was not printed, in the manner of a wife's, but inscribed as a handwritten side-note. A shiver ran down her spine. So she had been named after an ancestor. Her father had never mentioned the fact. Avidly she glanced at Natasha's dates. 1775 to 1860. The woman had lived to a ripe old age. But what had been her relationship to Regis? There were no de-tails. Just the scribbled note. How strange, she thought, flicking through the pages, that her namesake should be inscribed next to the name of the man nobody seemed to want to talk about.

After a while perusing the book, she felt sleep begin to press upon her, and, laying the volume down on an ornate table, she rose and yawned. Time to go upstairs and rest. Tomorrow she would seek further information.

As she wandered up the grand stairway Natasha glanced up at the portraits on the wall.

A lovely grey-eyed girl in a stiff brocade dress with a revealing décolleté—as had been the fashion in the late eighteenth century—stared down at her from one of them. Natasha held her breath as her eyes went to the tiny bronze plaque on the frame. As she'd supposed, it was Natasha de Saugure. Who had she married and had she been happy? she wondered suddenly. Her eyes in the portrait looked bright and filled with hope. But there was something else, a mysterious melancholic twist to the smile.

Natasha glanced at the painting a moment longer, then, letting out a sigh, she climbed the rest of the stairs and headed to her room.

CHAPTER FOUR

A WEEK passed and still Natasha hadn't taken any definite decision regarding her future. To her annoyance she experienced a moment's disappointment when there was no sign of Raoul at the end of the week. But she shook it off, reminding herself that it was for the best. He'd obviously seen the light, realized how embarrassing any involvement would be. After all, they might be neighbours for the next half-century for all she knew.

Neither had she had time to further her investigation into the lives of Regis d'Argentan and her ancestor Natasha, for Monsieur Dubois had appeared at the château the morning following her evening with Raoul, armed with heavy manila files overflowing with documents needing to be signed and filed, and others she needed to read to become familiar with her grandmother's estate.

'And you should visit your grandmother's apartment in Paris immediately,' the *notaire* had admonished in his precise legal tone.

So now here she was, a week later, sitting on a train headed to Paris.

Except for an old schoolfriend, she knew no one in that city. But, despite this somewhat daunting fact, Natasha was excited. Here she was, going to Paris to stay in her very own apartment. It seemed incredible. It was a long time since she'd visited the city with her parents, and the thought of rediscovering such exciting places as the Louvre and the Centre Pompidou, and ambling down the Champs Elysées, stopped her being anxious for long. Perhaps she would even hit Avenue Montaigne, now that she'd discovered the novel and intriguing delight of creating a new wardrobe.

As the train drew up to the platform at the Gare du Nord, Natasha stepped down with her practical roll-on case. She was about to follow the crowd down the platform towards the main station entrance when she heard her name called.

'Oh, my God,' she exclaimed as Raoul stood looming over her, his dark features stark in the afternoon sun. 'You gave me such a fright.'

'Forgive me. It was not my intention.'

'How did you know I was here?' she asked haughtily, hastily regaining her composure.

'I rang the Manoir to talk to you and Henri told me you'd be on the four-fifty, so I came to pick you up,' he replied matter-of-factly.

'Well, that's very nice of you,' she said, hoping her tone was dampening enough, and willing her pulse not to beat quite so hard, 'but Henri had no business telling you my whereabouts.' Another time she'd leave specific instructions not to reveal her plans.

'I think he assumed you would like to be picked up,' he said mildly, taking her case and slipping his hand protectively about her shoulders as two heavily laden backpackers nearly collided with her on the crowded platform. 'I believe you are not very familiar with Paris?'

'No, I'm not,' she acknowledged crossly, wishing she could calm the agitation that being next to him caused. Then, as they began walking down the platform, she saw Raoul signal to an older man in a grey suit and tie.

'May I introduce Pierre?' Raoul said smoothly, as they reached him. 'He drives for me. We shall be taking *mademoiselle* to the

Saugure apartment in the Place François Premier, Pierre.' His tone was polite, yet there was no doubt that the words were an order. Natasha felt strangely exhilarated and annoyed. How dared he swan into her life and simply take over? What if she'd wanted to go somewhere else rather than the apartment?

She was about to protest when by chance her eyes fell on the large queue waiting for taxis. It went against the grain, but she swallowed her words. It was really much simpler and more agreeable to be driven, even though Raoul's manner was intolerably high-handed. Of course she'd have to make it very plain indeed that she was not going to be herded around Paris at his pleasure, she reflected, climbing into the Bentley that had materialized as though by magic. She had her own plans for her Parisian stay, and they did not include Raoul d'Argentan.

Or at least they hadn't up until now.

'I thought you'd enjoy dining here,' Raoul said a few hours later as they glanced at their menus over the candlelit dinner table.

Natasha wasn't quite certain how she'd
ended up at Laurent's with Raoul. It had all
happened in such a natural manner that she'd
barely noticed the time go by. First she'd been
enchanted by the apartment, situated in one of
Paris's loveliest squares. It was ample, elegant,
and beautifully decorated. Very different from
the stiff formality of the Manoir, as though another hand had been at work here. The housekeeper, Madame Duvallier, a large middle-
aged woman with a warm smile and an
efficient manner, who had worked with the old
Comtesse for many years, had made her most
welcome. She'd also greeted Raoul warmly,
and it had been plain to Natasha that he was
an *habitué*.

Now, as they sat at the candlelit table, she
decided to question him. 'Have you come often to Grandmère's apartment?' she asked, after they'd ordered and the menus had been removed.

'Quite frequently. My parents and she were
friends. So, yes, I've been in and out over the
years. Lately the Comtesse had asked me for
some advice about her affairs. In fact, I'm
quite surprised she never told me that you were

to be her heir,' he added, with that same critical stare that left her feeling as though he was suspicious of her.

Natasha bristled. 'I don't see why she should have. After all, I didn't know myself.'

'No, but—' He cut off his words, shook his head and smiled. 'It is of no importance. Do not let us spoil such a pleasant evening by conjecturing over things which we cannot alter in any case.'

The logic of his argument struck home. There was little use in trying to figure out the old Comtesse's motives. She might as well do as he said, and enjoy the lovely atmosphere of the restaurant.

'Do you plan to make a long stay in Paris?' Raoul enquired as they sipped champagne, and Natasha felt a delicious headiness take hold of her.

'I really don't know. But very soon I'll have to decide whether or not I'm returning to my job. I took two months off. But after that I'll need to make a definite decision as to the future.'

'Do you enjoy your job?' he asked curiously, his eyes boring into hers.

'I do enjoy it, yes. It has been very fulfilling. But...' She hesitated, something stopping her from confiding in him.

'But?' He prodded gently, determined to get her to tell him what was on her mind.

'Well, it's just that all this has been so un-expected. I mean, how could I have imagined when I left Khartoum that my life would take such a strange turn?'

'No, you couldn't, could you?' he mur-mured, still sizing her up while accepting the caviar the waiter had placed before them. 'Now things seem very different?'

'Yes.' She hesitated, then decided to risk it and tell him how she felt. Expressing it might help her understand better herself. 'Now it's as though I have a new path that I must follow. Not that I'm certain yet,' she added hastily. 'It's too soon for me to take such a radical decision. The thing is that if I don't remain here—or at least at the Manoir—I'll probably have to sell it.'

'Sell the Manoir?' Raoul's cup hit the saucer with a crack. 'You can't sell the Manoir. It has been in the Saugure family for almost three centuries. The original house much longer than that. It's unthinkable.' His voice cut the air like a knife and his dark eyes flashed with anger.

'I know that. But all things have to move on at some point,' she reasoned thoughtfully.

'That is a ridiculous statement,' he bit back. 'Selling the Manoir is out of the question.'

'Might I remind you,' she said, drawing herself up, 'that it really is none of your business what I do with my property.'

'You can remind me as much as you like,' he answered, his burning eyes meeting hers full on in a clash of wills, 'but I assure you, *mademoiselle*, that I will personally make your life as difficult as possible should you even contemplate such an action. *Mon Dieu.* What would Marie Louise do if she could hear you? She must be turning in her grave at this very instant.' He sent her a withering look across the table and signalled the waiter for the bill.

'I don't see how you can stop me if I do decide to sell,' Natasha challenged, furious at his meddling. 'I have every right to do whatever I like with all three properties. Neither you nor anyone can stop me.'

'Technically I may not be able to stop you,' he replied in a low, menacing voice as the waiter approached, 'but I assure you that you would regret it if you so much as thought about selling the Manoir.'

'Are you threatening me?' Her chin jutted out and she faced him head on.

'Merely warning you that you are on shaky ground when it comes to selling. You have inherited a duty to your name and your lineage,' he threw, his tone as biting as it was derisive. 'Surely even an Englishwoman like you can understand that? Doesn't your bloodline mean anything to you?'

'You are insupportable,' Natasha hissed, throwing down her napkin on the table and getting up while the waiter hovered anxiously. 'I'll do whatever I like with my property, and I'll thank you to leave me alone. I need neither your assistance nor your advice. Goodnight.' On that dramatic note she swept regally from the table and made her way to the entrance of the restaurant.

When the doorman asked her if she wanted a cab she acquiesced gladly, still fuming from the altercation while desperately trying to ignore the needling truth that Raoul's words had brought home: she did feel a link to the past, and to her name and to all she owed it. But she was damned if she would admit that to him, she reflected savagely, letting out a cross huff as she waited impatiently for the cab.

So she had a temper. Well, he liked her all the better for it. But he was damned if he was going to let her get all sorts of ridiculous ideas into that pretty head of hers. Sell the Manoir indeed. Absurd. Plus, that might lead to the divulging of past history much better left buried.

Having settled the bill, Raoul made his way to the entrance of the restaurant, where he could see Natasha's back stiffly etched in the doorway. A smile hovered about his lips. She was turning out to be quite a handful, the drab little English miss. Not only had she been transformed into a raving beauty, but her character was proving more and more intriguing by the moment.

Signalling the doorman, he murmured to him to cancel the cab and approached Natasha.

'*Excusez-moi, mademoiselle*, if I said anything to offend you,' he murmured in a conciliatory tone, 'but the truth must be faced.'

She whirled around, eyes blazing. 'I've had just about enough of you for one evening, Raoul d'Argentan. Now, please leave me alone. I've ordered a cab and I can find my way back to the apartment perfectly well on my own.'

'But the doorman has just indicated to me that there are no taxis available in Paris at this hour,' he said, sounding much more French than he had before, and raising his hand in a very Gallic manner while shaking his head, eyes twinkling.

'Really? That wasn't the case five minutes ago,' she replied coldly.

'No? Well, things can change very fast in Paris. Transport is unreliable.' He slipped an arm into hers and began walking. 'Much better to let me accompany you—which, I might add, I do with pleasure.' The slight lilt of a French accent thickened and his eyes sparkled. 'Really, Natasha, there is no need to be upset. It is only a ride home, *après tout*, and you are only cross because I pointed out something that I have a funny feeling you already know deep down inside yourself.'

Natasha swallowed, bereft of words. How did he know? And how could she deny the truth? She glanced back at the doorman, who sent her an apologetic look. Anger still seethed inside her at the way she'd been so accurately read and cleverly manipulated. But, she realized, letting out a sigh, it was unlikely that the doorman would order her a cab now that the Baron had imposed his wretched will, and the best she could do, without causing an embarrassing scene, was to concede gracefully.

Several minutes later they drove alongside the Seine, past famous bridges, with the lights from the barges and *bateaux mouches* shimmering. On the Isle Saint-Louis she heard the chime of the bells at Nôtre Dame. It was impossible to be here, in this the loveliest of cities, and not surrender to its charm and enchantment.

'How about a drink before we turn in?' Raoul asked, taking a sidelong glance at her as he kept the car steady in the flow of traffic. She looked calmer, more composed. And he had no intention of letting her go home right now. She looked too beautiful in that silk dress, her hair flowing like golden wheat over her shoulders. Plus, he'd finally dispatched Clothilde and was therefore free as the wind. Added to all these valid reasons was the fact that the kiss they'd shared the other night in the car had remained strangely imprinted in his mind.

'I suggest we pop over to the bar of the Plaza Athénée. If you haven't been there before you'll find the decoration amusing.' He pulled his mobile out of his pocket, and before Natasha had a chance to agree or refuse he was reserving a table in quick French.

'Raoul, I never said I was going,' she said when he'd finished.

'Do you always have to protest against every good idea?' he countered with a shrug, a wicked smile breaking on his handsome face. 'Just relax—*voyons*—and go with the flow, as they say in America. After all, you're in Paris. Enjoy it.'

She sighed, realizing she was beaten and that actually she rather wanted to go for a drink. Plus, there really could be no possible harm in joining him in the bar of one of Paris's best hotels, she justified.

Soon they were seated in the corner of the dimly lit bar and Raoul ordered a bottle of Dom Perignon. The atmosphere was fun and young, and Natasha eyed the bar counter—a replica of a huge slab of ice, internally illuminated—intrigued.

'Like it?' Raoul asked, following her gaze.

'It's fun, isn't it? I like coming here.'

It was only then that he saw a slim familiar figure silhouetted across the room, seated with friends by the window, and his heart sank. Clothilde sat, sylphlike and languorously elegant, dressed as always in the latest Dior fashions. Her dark-eyed gaze fulminated as it rested upon him. Raoul glanced away. Why hadn't he remembered that she'd probably be here tonight? Hopefully she would be too proud to make a scene.

But his hopes were dashed when two minutes later Clothilde snaked between the tables, her slim hips swaying, then stood before him, her long black hair shrouding her face, a cigarette waving in her nervous fingers.

'Monsieur le Baron,' she threw sarcastically, 'to what do we owe the pleasure of your pres-

ence here tonight? I thought you were rural-
izing for a while.'

'Good evening, Clothilde. May I introduce
an English friend of mine, Natasha de
Saugure?'

'*Non!*' Clothilde exclaimed. 'I'm not interested in your friends or your lies,' she spat
venomously, sending Natasha a scathing look.
'You're a liar and a cheat, Raoul d'Argentan,
and I'll make sure all of Paris knows it. Be
careful of him,' she added, addressing Natasha,
'he's the biggest bastard in town.' Then, tossing her head, she turned on her spiky high
heels and stalked back to her table, where her
cohorts sat watching approvingly.

Raoul sighed and shook his head. 'Sorry
about that,' he murmured. 'I'm afraid
Clothilde is rather theatrical.'

'Who is she? Your girlfriend?'

'Ex-girlfriend. If you can call her that. I
dated her for a while and she thought it was
more serious than it ever was. Why is it that
women always fall into that trap?' he enquired,
brows knit. 'I don't understand why they can't
just accept the *status quo* and enjoy it. It al-

ways amazes me how they complicate life.' He shook his head and let out a sigh.

'Perhaps the women you run into have a deeper sense of commitment than you do,' she replied, tongue in cheek, before taking a sip of chilled champagne.

'Maybe. But no commitment ever existed in the first place. Not on my side anyway. I made that abundantly plain from the outset.'

'But things can start out as casual in life and then become deeper as time goes on,' Natasha argued.

He shrugged in what she considered to be a very French gesture. 'I never make promises that I might break. And I never offered marriage or even an in-house living arrangement to Clothilde. I really don't see why she's so upset.'

'Well, *she* seems to think she has a ton of reasons,' Natasha remarked tartly.

'You see?' He turned and threw his hands up. 'That is exactly what I mean. Women are all the same—always filling in the blanks with all sorts of reasons and justifications for getting their own way. I will never understand them.'

Natasha smothered a smile and decided there was little point in pursuing the subject. But Clothilde's burst of anger had left her thinking. It was clear that Raoul was a seasoned playboy, used to getting his own way. Perhaps she should take the other woman's warning seriously. After all, she knew nothing about him except that he was her neighbour in Normandy.

Later, as they drove back to the apartment through the quiet streets of the city, she determined to keep her distance from this man. She'd learned her lesson with Paul, hadn't she? The minute you trusted you could also be betrayed. And, frankly, she had very few reasons to trust Raoul.

When they reached the imposing building he stopped the car and parked. 'How about inviting me in for a nightcap?' he said with a grin.

'I don't think so. I'm quite tired tonight. I have a long day tomorrow—meetings with my grandmother's lawyers and so on.'

'Ah, you're meeting with Perret, I take it.' He nodded. 'He's quite a good man on the whole, but I told Marie Louise she might want to consider a change of legal counsel.'

'And why is that?'

'Oh, I'll tell you some other time, when you have more time on your hands,' he answered affably.

Natasha could have kicked herself for falling into the trap.

'Right—well, I'd better be going.' She began opening the door, but he leaned quickly across her and held it closed.

'Not so fast, *ma belle*,' he murmured, his voice turning husky. 'You can't be in that much of a hurry.'

'I—' Natasha felt her body click into overdrive. What was it about this man that left her mesmerized, unable to react as she should? When his hand slipped behind her neck and he drew her close, his lips dropping a trail of deliciously feathery kisses on her cheek, down past her lips, her throat, then slipped to her breast, instead of repulsing him she let out a pent-up sigh of longing.

It was as though her mind had blurred and her normal functions simply didn't work. She knew she should react, knew it was ridiculous to allow him this liberty, but as his fingers expertly caressed her taut nipples and his lips ravaged her mouth with such intense desire it was impossible to resist. Inside she felt a new and strange sensation, the same as she'd felt the other night, as though he'd pressed an invisible button over which he had complete control. His fingers slipped under her top and she gasped as skin met skin and his skilled fingers taunted further, making her writhe, leaving her conscious of a deeper yearning, a need for further fulfilment, that left her aching and damp, longing to throw caution to the winds and let him have his way.

But finally reason asserted itself and she withdrew reluctantly from his embrace. Righting her clothes, Natasha said in a shaky voice, 'I think it's better if we don't see each other any more. This—this shouldn't be happening. I—we're neighbours. We shouldn't— What I mean is—'

Raoul laid his hand over hers and leaned back in the soft cream leather seat. 'Are you afraid, Natasha?'

'I—I don't know. It's all too fast. Too much has happened to me in the past few days. I can't keep up.'

'You mean you're scared of enjoying your-self?' he queried, a subtle knowing smile hovering about his lips. 'My dear, what is wrong with seeking pleasure?'

'Look, I can't handle this, okay?' she said, suddenly upset, tears of frustration and confusion burning as she grappled for the car door handle. 'I want to go.'

'Then of course you shall,' he said quietly, eyeing her, a slight frown entering his eyes. He had not expected this reaction from her.

Quickly Raoul stepped out of the vehicle and opened the door. 'I'll say goodnight and *au revoir*, then, but not goodbye. We will see each other, and if you don't want me to kiss you then I won't,' he said, touching her cheek in a tender gesture. 'But don't get upset. It was just a nice interlude for both of us. *Sans plus,*' he added lightly.

'Right.' Natasha swallowed and took a deep breath.

'I'll give you a call. Maybe I can take you to see some of the sights you may want to enjoy. We could go out to the country for lunch one day.'

This was said in a firm, friendly tone, and Natasha wondered if she'd been dreaming. Had this same man who was now casually saying goodnight held her in his arms so passionately only moments before?

Once inside the building Natasha entered the elevator, sank against the wall, and let out a relieved sigh. Yet it was impossible to deny the internal havoc she was experiencing, the molten desire still throbbing in places she had never before been wholly conscious of. She really must get away from Raoul before she made a complete fool of herself, she reflected, biting her lower lip. Perhaps after the meetings tomorrow she would head down to the South of France and visit her grandmother's villa, near the village of Eze, above Monte Carlo. That would give her time to breathe, to understand better all that had occurred over the past few days, help her to take the decisions that eventually must be faced.

On reaching her floor, she entered the apartment and closed the door carefully behind her. So much had happened so fast and it was hard to keep up. And the roiling feelings caused by the moments spent in Raoul's arms were as perturbing as all the rest.

If not more so.

CHAPTER FIVE

THE meeting with Monsieur Perret proved to be long and rather boring. He went over and over several deeds and papers, leaving Natasha wondering if perhaps Raoul wasn't right, and that more efficient legal counsel might be found. But for now all she wanted was to escape Paris and the proximity of the dangerous Baron. It was most degrading to think that he merely had to touch her to cause her to react as though she'd been lit by a damned match, that a mere kiss and a flick of his skilled fingers could make her quiver like a jelly. It was shaming. Made her wonder just what kind of a woman she was.

But even as she packed her bag, determined to get on the TGV as soon as possible, Natasha found herself unable to banish the previous evening as summarily as she would have liked. She simply must exercise more control over herself, she reflected, zipping the suitcase. Imagine if this happened to her the minute any

man touched her! Yet why had it never occurred with Paul? she wondered as she entered
a taxi and made her way through the busy
Parisian streets to the station.

Once on the train, Natasha sat next to the
window and read the paper, determined not to
allow Raoul and his magnetic aura to occupy
her thoughts. She was dealing with so many
new factors in her life. The last thing she
needed was to be distracted by silly nonsense.

Several hours later the train arrived in Nice,
and she took a taxi up to the medieval village
of Eze. The stunning Mediterranean villa stood
on a small plateau, caught between sea and
mountain. It was spectacular, and had main-
tained all of its original character, and Natasha
knew at once that this was one spot she would
not let go of easily. It was as if she immediately identified with the place.

Madame Bursin, the housekeeper, had prepared a lovely room, decorated in pale blues
and whites. And all at once time rolled back
and Natasha recalled her father telling her of
wonderful summers spent here in his youth.
She experienced a rush of nostalgia. What a
pity it was that her grandmother had banished

them so definitively from her life. They could have spent such wonderful times here together.

But there was little use regretting the past, and instead she changed into a brief white bikini and headed out towards the cerulean pool that overlooked the glistening Mediterranean below, dotted with yachts and small craft. It was a sight she knew she would never tire of.

Lying down on a *chaise-longue*, Natasha sighed and smiled. She felt better now, more in control. And even proud of herself. She'd escaped Raoul's clutches and could go back to being her own person. Now all she had to do was relax, think about her life and how it was going to shape up, and she'd be well on her way.

'What do you mean she left?' Raoul asked crossly.

'I'm afraid she's gone, Monsieur le Baron. She left this morning after her meetings with Monsieur Perret.'

'And did she say where she was going?' Raoul drummed irritated fingers on the sleek teak desk of his Paris office and cradled the phone against his shoulder. This was not going according to plan.

'No. I'm afraid *mademoiselle* didn't say.'

'Thank you.' He hung up abruptly and swung around in the black leather chair, his expression foreboding. She was running away from him. The thought both annoyed and intrigued him. Women never ran away from him. Rather they invented pathetic excuses to see him again. Raoul stopped swinging and sat up straight. He must find out where she was. Though why the hell it mattered he hadn't fathomed yet. Perhaps it was just the fact that he didn't like being thwarted. And, although he knew it was not strictly wise, he knew he had every intention of having an affair with Natasha. Or at least taking her to bed a few times to satisfy his desire for her. He had the feeling they would both enjoy that. And she knew it. He *knew* that she knew it. Could tell by her reactions, the way she moved in his arms, the way her body turned pliant and receptive the minute he grazed her breast. So why run? Why not stay and enjoy it?

He let out a long huff and shook his head. Women were, as he'd remarked only last night after Clothilde's little display of hysterics, incomprehensible. But that didn't help him.

As the morning drifted by he felt increasingly frustrated that there was no phone call, no indication at all of Natasha's whereabouts. By midday he was impatiently ringing the Manoir, where he met with another negative.

So she hadn't gone back there.

Had she returned to England? he wondered, glancing at his watch, aware that he was expected at the Relais Plaza in half an hour, for lunch with his cousin Madeleine.

Precisely on time, he entered the restaurant and was greeted by name by the head waiter, who immediately showed him to a table by the window on the banquette. Two minutes later Madeleine, a chic, attractive Parisian woman of his own age, entered the restaurant and he rose to greet her. Soon they were settled and sipping champagne.

'So, *mon vieux*, how is life treating you?' she asked, sending him an amused smile across the table.

'Not too bad. That is to say, did you hear of the death of Marie Louise de Saugure?'

'Actually, yes. I read the obituary. I meant to come up for the funeral but I got caught up with Frederic's exams. Tell me about it.'

'Oh, very impressive—old retainers lining the road as the hearse went by. Just as it should have been.'

'God, you're so medieval,' she remarked, shaking her head and sighing gustily. 'Just like our ancestor Regis, I'll bet, and just as wicked.'

'That is pure speculation.'

'Is it? I wonder if his lover thought so,' she mused.

'The beautiful Natasha?'

'Yes. I've always wondered why those two never married. It always struck me as so silly. All because of false pride. Men are so stupid.'

'What rubbish you talk, Madeleine.'

'Maybe, but the legend has always intrigued me. She was very beautiful, if the portrait at the Manoir is anything to go by. She should have used that to snare him.'

'What an idea. He would never have conceded.' Raoul suddenly remembered the portrait and his eyes narrowed. Damned if it didn't resemble the present Natasha.

'I shall miss Marie Louise and her acerbic remarks,' Madeleine said with a sigh as she glanced through the menu. 'She was a wonderful old lady—although I remember when I used to quake in my shoes whenever we went over to the Manoir when we were children. Now, tell me, who inherits?'

'An English granddaughter,' he replied blandly. 'How about some *foie gras*?'

'You don't say? I'd forgotten the Comtesse had a son she disinherited.'

'She did. He was considerably older than us, which is why we don't remember him well. He married unsuitably. An Englishwoman of no consequence. The Comtesse was very *fâchée*.'

'And cut him out of her will?'

'Exactly. He was disinherited. But apparently she changed her mind shortly before her death. And now the granddaughter, who never even knew her and arrived for a visit only hours before her death, has inherited everything.'

'Well. What a story. And what is her name?'

'Natasha.'

'Excuse me?' Madeleine put her glass down with a snap and their eyes met. 'You can't be serious. Natasha? But surely no one in that family would adopt the name after—well, after what happened.'

'I wouldn't have thought so.' He shrugged. 'Either Hubert de Saugure had a warped sense of humour or he wanted to thwart his mother.'

'Natasha,' Madeleine mused thoughtfully. 'I've often wondered why she did what she did, damaging both our families so completely. She must have loved Regis very much. It all happened so long ago, yet the shadow of her ghost seems to linger, doesn't it?'

'Frankly, I've never considered the matter.'

'How typical. Still, it has to be more than a coincidence.'

'A surprising course of events, I admit, but don't let's stretch our imaginations too far.'

'Tell me, what's she like, this English girl?' Madeleine asked, intrigued. 'How old is she?'

'Young. About twenty-three. She is an interesting young woman who has spent the past few years in Africa doing humanitarian work.'

'Goodness.' Madeleine's brows flickered. 'That sounds dreadfully righteous.'

'Not at all. I get the impression of an intelligent and sensitive human being.' He couldn't explain why, but it annoyed him that his cousin should dismiss Natasha in such a callous manner.

'Oh? So you've talked to her in depth?' A mischievous smile similar to his own curved Madeleine's expressive lips. 'Already smitten, *mon cousin*?'

'Rubbish. But I have had occasion to speak with her, yes. Naturally I went over there to offer my condolences.'

'Naturally.' She nodded, her flashing eyes belying her words. 'Raoul, *chéri*, this is *me* you're talking to—your old devoted playmate who knows you like the back of her hand. And all I have to say is that it would be the first time in history that you went to see any young woman unless she was minimally attractive.'

'Really, Madeleine,' he murmured, his lips quivering, 'you underestimate me.'

'So I presume,' she continued, ignoring him, 'that your new neighbour is at the very least gorgeous?' She quirked a brow and waited.

'She's attractive,' he conceded, reluctant to say more lest Madeleine make the wrong assumptions. 'Frankly, at first I thought she was a dowd. But she seems to have had some sort of make-over. Quite surprising, really. Now, why don't we order?' he said picking up the menu and signalling the waiter. 'I hear the *filets de sole meunière* are excellent today.'

Madeleine opened her mouth, about to say more, then decided against it. Something told her that perhaps she shouldn't meddle this time. So with good grace she picked up the menu and made her choice.

When by that evening Raoul still had no news of Natasha—and to his annoyance found it hard to concentrate on anything else—he decided he must take measures to ensure his comfort. He was damned if he was going to let her disturb his equilibrium in this manner. He wanted her—wanted to bed her. And that was exactly what he intended to do.

It was only next morning when he woke up that he remembered Marie Louise's villa in Eze and sat up in bed with a start. '*Voilà,*' he exclaimed, snapping his fingers. 'I'll bet that's where she's hiding out.

Minutes later he was up and packing an overnight bag. After a quick croissant and *café au lait* at the brasserie on the corner of his street he jumped in the car and headed south on the autoroute. It would take several hours to reach Eze, but he wasn't in a hurry. He had advised his office that he would be absent for a couple of days, and only to contact him on his mobile in case of an emergency.

Raoul loved a good chase, and this was certainly turning into one. A better one than he'd been offered in a while. Of late his women seemed to comply all too boringly with his every wish. And thus they bored him.

But Natasha certainly didn't do that.

She felt deliciously calm here at the Villa Le Caprice, Natasha decided, letting out a long, delighted sigh. Even though it wasn't that hot as yet, she found lying by the pool relaxing, reading or simply thinking about the future, an ideal occupation. It allowed her to put into perspective everything that lay before her. She must, she realized, find out more about her family's history. It intrigued her now. As though part of her had been missing all these years. She particularly wanted to learn the tale of Regis d'Argentan and how he was connected to the Saugures. There appeared to be a mystery connected to him and her family, and she had every intention of finding out what that mystery was. She wished now that instead of letting herself go all gooey in Raoul's arms she'd spent the time more productively, finding out about her ancestry.

The thought of Raoul—who, if she was truthful, was never far from her mind—made her swallow. What a good thing she'd taken the decision to leave Paris. Thank God she was sensible at heart. Feeling a slight sense of pride at having exercised self-control, despite the longing images that flashed regularly before her at the mere thought of him, Natasha decided that today she would wander further afield. Her grandmother had a wonderful 1960s convertible Rolls, and she couldn't resist the temptation of taking it out for a spin. Madame Bursin and her husband Jacques were everything that was kind and helpful, and the car had been taken to the garage to make sure it was in excellent working order. Now she couldn't wait.

The day was perfect, with a blue cloudless sky and sparkling sea below. Having donned a pair of white capri pants and a pretty matching top, Natasha put on her sunglasses and tied back her hair, feeling positively like a fifties movie star. Tossing her large handbag on the passenger seat, she was about to get into the vehicle when she heard the rumble of an engine.

Standing up straighter, she stiffened. Surely it couldn't be him. Yet there he was, cruising up her drive in that damn sports car of his, as cool as you please. She should have left orders not to let him in. But, she realized, as the vehicle drew up and Jacques hastened towards it, he probably had this lot under his thumb as well.

Knowing she could not make a scene in front of the servants, Natasha pulled herself together and tried to look dignified.

'Well,' she remarked, ignoring her racing pulse once he'd exited the car, 'what are you doing here?' She hoped to God she looked more poised and sophisticated than she felt.

'I think you know exactly why I'm here,' he answered in a low husky voice as he leaned over to peck her cheek, leaving her no option but to submit to this form of address.

The attractive sight of him dressed in designer trousers, a loose sports shirt and loafers with a navy jersey casually thrown over his shoulders, had not escaped her, and she swallowed bravely, determined not to let him faze her.

'I can't think what can have brought you here,' she replied in what she hoped was a nonchalant tone. 'In fact, you're very lucky to have caught me as I was about to go for a spin.'

'But please don't let me stop you,' he insisted, stepping around the car and opening the door for her. 'It will be my pleasure to be your guide.'

'I wasn't aware I needed one.'

'Oh, but surely, *ma chère*, you don't imagine I would abandon you. It would be too callous of me to allow a young woman on her own—the granddaughter of an old family friend, I might add—to venture alone onto the Riviera without my assistance.' He demurred, eyes sparkling with mischief, as he held the door.

'Oh, do stop talking such rot and rubbish,' she exclaimed, caught between amusement and irritation and the chills coursing down her spine. 'I'm perfectly capable of taking care of myself, I'll have you know. I don't need a chaperon.'

'Ah, but that is where you are wrong. All women need a chaperon—especially beautiful wealthy ones. There are always unscrupulous young men out to make a buck.' He tut-tutted, grinned devastatingly at her and held out his hand. 'Let's call a truce, fair Natasha. I shan't bother you, merely try to be a friend? Okay? You agree?' He smiled winningly now, leaving her no alternative but to shrug and slide behind the wheel with as much grace as she could muster.

CHAPTER SIX

IT WAS impossible not to melt, impossible not to surrender to the enchantment of enjoying the South of France with such a handsome, suave escort.

Raoul knew everything and everybody. They were received in restaurants by name, accompanied by obsequious head waiters to the best tables, and attended to in the best possible manner. How, Natasha wondered dolefully as they returned on their third evening to the villa, could she simply go back to her old life and pick up where she'd left off?

And all at once she knew that it would be impossible.

Sad as it made her feel, she could not go back to Africa.

That part of her life was over and a new chapter was opening before her. For a moment she glanced through the shadows at Raoul, then concentrated on driving up the Corniche back to the villa. He had not, she reflected ruefully, so much as tried to kiss her again. In fact, he'd been so platonic she almost wished he would. Somehow staving him off was a lot more satisfying than wondering why he hadn't made the attempt.

As she drew the car up on the gravel Raoul leaned coolly back into the corner of the passenger seat and watched her. He would let her stew just a little longer, he decided, an amused smile curving his lips through the darkness. She was delightful, his little English miss, but he wanted her on his terms: wanting him. To the point where he could twist his little finger and put into practice some of the many fantasies that had crossed his mind during the past few nights. If truth be told, sleep had come with difficulty. It was not until the early hours that Raoul had encountered peace on his pillow. Now he had no desire for peace. Rather, he wished he could give vent to the strong longing coursing through him. But it was too soon. He needed her to give him that subtle, undefined signal which meant he'd won.

And to his utter annoyance it hadn't come.

When was the last time he'd waited three whole days for a woman to submit to his advances? He couldn't even recall. It was absurd, ridiculous, and he was very nearly losing his patience. But wait he must, or she would have the upper hand. And that, he realized ruefully, he couldn't allow. And then, too, there was something about Natasha herself that stopped him from taking the action he would nor-mally—something he had rarely encountered before in a woman. Not obstinacy, not petu-lance or selfish desire, which were traits of many of the women he'd dated, but rather a sense of purpose to her life that he found in-triguing. They had spent several hours talking about the future, about her plans. He'd sensed her initial reluctance to stay in France, her doubts about whether she should go back to her job or stay in what would be a comfortable and easy lifestyle. And knew from the start that she was seeking something more.

A woman with a purpose in her life.

This was definitely a new breed of female he had rarely encountered. Oh, he'd met enough ambition in his time to recognize that—the calculating style of women deter-mined to claw their way up the social or pro-fessional ladder at whatever cost. But Natasha had no such intention. It was as though she was seeking a deeper motivation to make her decision. As though she needed to know what her purpose in France was before she could choose it.

Raoul opened the car door and got out. He felt strangely confused, annoyed with himself and suddenly with her for placing him on this new untrodden territory. He didn't like being on unfamiliar terrain. Perhaps it was time to leave, shake off this strange spell Natasha had cast over him and return to Paris.

He watched as she stepped out of the vehicle, then together they made their way back into the silent villa and moved towards the terrace.

'A nightcap?' he suggested casually.

'No, thanks.' She shook her head and headed towards the French windows and the terrace. The moon shone full and bright over the shimmering waters of the Mediterranean; the lights of the gin palaces twinkled merrily. Natasha sat on the balustrade and gazed down at them, trying to sum up the past few days, to escape the awareness of Raoul's physical presence: so close, so tempting, so alluring.

She was dying to give in to him, to submit to his intense male allure, to all the feelings throbbing inside her. But something stopped her.

She looked up as he came to join her, a snifter of cognac in his hand.

'I shall be returning to Paris tomorrow,' he remarked in that languid tone that left her no clue as to what he felt. She felt a stab and swallowed. How was it possible that in these few short days she'd grown so used to his presence?

'Of course,' she replied, hiding her dismay. What would it be like to be here alone? It was almost as if France and Raoul had become synonymous. Which was ridiculous, she chided herself. She simply must pull herself together and face reality. She had decisions to make. Life-changing decisions. And she needed all her wits about her to make them.

'You don't mind?' He quirked an eyebrow in her direction. 'I had the impression we were getting on rather well, you and I.' He poised a loafered foot on the balustrade and swirled his cognac thoughtfully.

'I think we've spent a very pleasant time,' she said, her voice non-committal lest she betray any feelings.

'A pleasant time?' he remarked, letting out a laugh. 'That is so cool, so very British. I would rather say that we have spent *des moments formidables*. But then I'm French.' He looked down at her speculatively. 'Are you sure this was nothing but a *pleasant time*, Natasha? Are you really able to deny the intense attraction we feel for one another?'

'I—' She clasped her hands, confused by his direct attack.

'You what?' He slipped onto the balustrade next to her, his proximity leaving her in intense turmoil.

'I don't know. I just think, well, that—'

'Stop thinking. One of your problems is that you think too much, *ma chère*. This is about feeling, not thinking.'

The glass was abandoned and his arms closed about her as he drew her up to standing position and folded her in them. 'Stop thinking, Natasha,' he growled into her ear. 'Just feel—feel everything I have to give you.'

She stood stiffly for a moment, then, unable to resist, gave way as his mouth found hers. The kiss was long and sensuous, his tongue investigating her mouth slowly while his hand slipped down her back and cupped her bottom, pressing her against him firmly, so that she felt the hardness of him pressed temptingly against her. Her breasts felt suddenly taut and aching, that strange new tingle throbbing between her thighs so strong and so compelling that instinctively she pressed herself harder against him. Then Raoul's expert fingers trailed down her throat and reached the tip of her aching breast. Natasha threw her head back and let out a sigh of contentment as his fingers grazed the taut peaks, taunting her tender nipples, before reaching further down, down, until he slipped beneath her panties and penetrated the warm, damp softness.

'No, Raoul, please,' she begged weakly. She mustn't let him do this—could not let herself be dominated by this man and her own uncontrolled desire. But she had never experienced anything like it before. She was swooped into a new, terrifying landscape that both frightened and enthralled her.

'Just relax, *chérie*,' he whispered, his fingers caressing her now, causing tiny gasps to escape her lips as his thumb grazed and his fingers penetrated. 'Ah, you are delicious, my Natasha, as delicious as I thought you would be.'

'Raoul,' she whispered, between a plea and a protest. Then, when she least expected it, something extraordinary happened. The tight, anxious throbbing and the incredibly tense build-up that she'd thought she could stand no more gave way, and she let out a long gasp of sheer satisfaction, laced with utter amazement.

It was staggering.

Blissful.

Incredible.

As though a window had opened in her life.

And as she leaned against him, caught in the throes of her first orgasm, Raoul smiled and held her close, pride and triumph rushing through him as he sensed her utter surprise. So she had never experienced this before. He leaned her head against his chest and held her close, feeling the fast throbbing of her heart, quelling his own intense desire as he gazed out over the sea, breathed in the scent of lavender and listened to the crickets' endless chorus filling the night.

'Come,' he said softly, when he felt she'd regained her equilibrium. 'We must finish this off properly, *ma mie.*' He slipped his arms under her and swept her into them.

'But Raoul, please—this isn't—I mean, I don't want—'

He stopped a moment, looked at her with eyes brimming with humour. 'Are you seriously telling me you don't want me, Natasha?' he asked, gazing down at her amused.

'I—it's not that I don't want you,' she whispered hoarsely. 'I just don't feel ready to.'

How she'd managed to retain enough sanity to utter those words she had no idea. But somewhere in the back of her mind a little voice told her that were she to allow Raoul to make love to her tonight it would in some way destroy her.

He hesitated a moment. 'You are talking nonsense,' he said, holding her firmly in his arms. 'Why can't you just close your eyes and enjoy all the pleasure I can give you? Surely you have not had such a bad time this evening?' he coaxed, the knowing smile still playing about his lips.

'Please. Let me down.' It was impossible to reason with him being held in his arms.

Reluctantly Raoul conceded. Once she was standing, Natasha raked trembling fingers through her hair and tried to regain some composure. 'Raoul, I can't. It's not that I don't want to. It's just that I don't feel confident enough.'

'Leave that to me, *chérie*. I realize that you are new at this game, that you have little experience in matters of love. But have no fear, *ma belle*. I have enough for both of us.'

'That's exactly what bothers me,' she retorted, suddenly recovering some of her lost poise. 'I don't plan to be an amusing pastime for you. I'm well aware that it must be intriguing for you to come across an inexperienced bumpkin like me. It may even amuse you to teach me a few things. For a while.'

'And what is wrong with that?' he asked, dropping his hands possessively on her shoulders. 'Think of it as part of furthering your education. Learning the art of lovemaking can be deliciously satisfying, and it will serve you well in the future,' he replied confidently.

'Really?' Natasha pulled away, suddenly clear in her mind as to why she did not want things to go any further. 'Surprising though this may seem to you, Raoul, I don't think of lovemaking either as an art-form or a game. You said you were leaving for Paris tomorrow. I think it's a good thing that you are. We obviously have far less in common than our conversations of the past few days have led us to believe. Now, if you'll excuse me, I'll say goodnight.'

Before he could stop her Natasha had turned on her heel and hastened up the stairs, head high, leaving Raoul fuming in the hall, wondering how what had appeared to be developing into a deliciously seductive evening had so suddenly turned sour.

'Damn her,' he muttered, returning to the terrace, where he downed the rest of his cognac. 'Damn all women.'

And this one was nothing but a little teaser.

Well, he'd had enough. Had wasted too much time on her already. He had a life to live, a business and an estate to run, didn't he? It was high time he got back in gear and stopped fooling around like a raw teenager.

In a few masterful strides he marched to his bedroom on the ground floor, threw his belongings into his Vuitton luggage and, closing the door behind him, made his way to his Ferrari. He would leave not tomorrow morning but right now. He'd had enough of Mademoiselle de Saugure and her silly infantile games, thank you very much.

Natasha sat trembling on the edge of the large canopied bed. Her head shot up when she heard the sound of the engine and the crunch of wheels on the gravel.

So he'd left.

Her hands dropped in her lap and she let out a sigh of mixed relief and regret. But it was better like this, she argued, and she was right to have held back. No good could come of a hot, passionate affair with Raoul. He'd become bored with her as quickly as he'd become attracted. Clothilde's words still lingered in her ears. 'He's the biggest bastard in town.' She had no doubt that Clothilde was right. So why, when she should be feeling nothing but relief at her escape, was she feeling so down?

Probably because they'd got on so well these past few days, she justified, slipping off her dress and underwear and reaching for her nightgown. Still, as she lay between the cool linen sheets it was impossible not to recall the overwhelming sensations she'd experienced. Natasha sighed, turned on her side, and tried to sleep. But her dreams were fraught with images of a tall dark man on a chestnut horse, swooping her up into the saddle, his hand poised possessively on her breast.

And her sleep was troubled.

CHAPTER SEVEN

'So, as I was telling you, Monsieur Dubois, I have decided to remain here in France and assume my grandmother's responsibilities.'

'This is wonderful news, *mademoiselle*,' Monsieur Dubois replied, beaming. 'The people on the estate will be thrilled to know that they will not be dealing with an absentee landowner.'

'No, they won't. I plan to learn as much about the estate as possible,' Natasha supplied with a smile as, seated behind the large desk in the Manoir's office, she flipped through some papers. 'And I also want to learn as much as possible about the history of the place. It is, after all, my heritage. I feel I should be familiar with every aspect of it, both historical and practical.'

'But of course, of course, *chère mademoiselle*. We shall be only too glad to inform you. I personally can tell you about the legal ramifications of the estate, but you must meet with Evreux, the factor. He will be able to fill you in on the happenings on the land. And as for history—well, I can think of no one better than Monsieur le Curé, down in the village. He is a very learned man, and a historian as well as a priest. He has spent thirty-five years in our parish and knows more about the place than anyone I know. Excluding Madame Blanchard, of course.'

'Madame Blanchard?' Natasha asked curiously, the name seeming familiar.

'Yes. She is the housekeeper over at Argentan. She works for the Baron, you know. Has done so all her life. I believe she went as a young kitchen maid before the war. She knows all the anecdotes there are to know. Particularly about yours and the Baron's families.'

'Why is that?' Natasha asked, frowning.

'Well, it is said…' Monsieur Dubois looked furtively about, then lowered his voice as though the walls might hear what he was about to say, 'that *madame*'s father was the issue of an affair between the Baron's grandfather and a village girl. So in some way she is related to the Argentans, and rather proud of it.'

'I see.' And she did—only too well. The Argentans certainly didn't waste their time, she reflected dryly, thankful for her moment's sanity in Eze, which had stopped her from falling victim to the present Baron's ploys. 'I shall look forward to meeting all these people. But first we must go over the details you have prepared for me.'

'*Avec plaisir, mademoiselle.*' Monsieur Dubois smiled broadly and took out a thick sheaf of papers, and Natasha prepared to begin her first lesson in how to run an estate.

So she'd decided to stay in France after all.

Raoul felt both elated and annoyed. Her presence represented both a challenge and a source of failure. He was surprised that she had assumed her role as châtelaine of the Manoir. After all, she'd appeared very hesitant. But he was fast learning—to his exasperation—that there was a hell of a lot more to Natasha de Saugure than met the eye.

Well, so much the better. At least he'd learned in time. By now Raoul was thoroughly convinced that it was *he* who had extracted himself from Natasha's wiles. The fact that she had summarily dismissed him had been relegated to the confines of his brain, where it remained safely secluded and could not damage his ego. Still, the thought that he was driving back to Argentan this weekend, and would spend the whole three days there without knowing what she was up to, was profoundly irritating.

Never mind, he reflected, banishing the thought, he had the races to attend this weekend. After all, it was mid-August, and the Prix Morny was being run in Deauville on Sunday. He had other fish to fry instead of worrying about Mademoiselle de Saugure. And he had a horse running. A pretty serious contender, too, for that matter. He just hoped the terrain wouldn't be too soft, as it had rained most of the week. Perhaps he should invite someone to attend the races with him in his box.

For several minutes Raoul sat behind his desk and flipped pensively through a small black address book. But none of the names he studied held any appeal. Better, he decided, to go back to the Château d'Argentan and ring his local friends when he arrived. Plus, Madeleine and her husband might be staying in their lovely property near Falaise. He would pop over and visit them. Perhaps they would like to join him in his box on Sunday.

Several hours later Raoul drew up into the medieval courtyard where Jean, the butler, was moving forward to greet him.

'Hello, Jean,' he said, as the butler picked his bag off the leather seat in the back of the Range Rover.

'*Bienvenu*, Monsieur le Baron.'

'So. How are things? Anything to report?' he asked as they made their way to the huge oak front door.

'Nothing much, *monsieur*, except the latest news that has the whole village in a buzz.'

'What's that?'

'Mademoiselle de Saugure has come to live at the Manoir.'

'I'd heard,' he responded shortly.

'Yes. It is exciting, isn't it? All the people on the estate are very happy about it. Apparently *mademoiselle* has taken a great interest in their lives. She has visited all the families personally and is already implementing a number of measures which they've been trying unsuccessfully to get the old Comtesse to put into practice for years.' Jean smiled broadly, glad to be the bearer of good tidings.

'Well, isn't that interesting?' Raoul mused. 'So she plans to make this her permanent home, I gather?'

'Apparently so, *monsieur*. I met Monsieur le Curé at the village tobacconist yesterday and he was singing her praises. Apparently she is most interested in local history and has asked him to fill her in. You know how the Curé loves to go on about the past. He is delighted. He even asked when you were coming as he wants to borrow some old documents from your library.'

'Really?' Raoul's brows flew up and his face closed. 'I shall have to call him, then, won't I?'

Without another word he swung through the door and marched straight to his study, leaving Jean wondering what he had said to provoke his master's ill humour. With a shrug he made his way upstairs, shaking his head. There was just no understanding the aristocracy.

It was both exciting and confusing, and it was a lot to absorb in such a short time. But now that she'd taken the definite decision to stay Natasha had thrown herself wholeheartedly into the task of learning her new role. Not an easy one, she'd realized after studying all that needed to be repaired, listening to complaints and hopes for the future, trying to understand some of the trials that working a thirty-five-hour week implied, and becoming familiar with French employment laws. Of course Monsieur Dubois and the factor, Evreux, took care of most of these aspects of the running of the property, but she was determined to familiarize herself with the details and not be dependent only on the knowledge of others.

That Friday evening she was glad to soak in a bath, slip on a comfy tracksuit and curl in front of the fire in the *petit salon*—the one place in the house that was remotely homey—and watch television. As she glanced about her Natasha realized that her next task would be to undertake some redecorating. She simply could not survive surrounded by such stiff formality, and she already had a better idea of how she'd like the place to look. When she had some time she would pop down to Paris and meet with a couple of designers to see who would be most suited to the task.

Not that time was something she had much of. Meetings and work seemed never-ending now that she'd plunged into the thick of it. Also there were social calls to be paid. The neighbours—excepting Raoul, who hadn't shown any sign of life since her return—were charming. In fact Philippe, son of the Comte de Morrieux, a rather pasty-faced, stiff young man, with sandy hair and very precise speech, had asked her to accompany him and his parents to the races this weekend. At first she'd been inclined to refuse. But then she'd realized that not only would it be fun to go to the famous races in Deauville, but that it might seem churlish and rude to refuse the kind invitation. She just hoped she had something suitable to wear among her new acquisitions. She'd been relieved when she'd learned that she wouldn't be expected to wear a hat.

As she flipped through the TV channels Natasha mentally summed up her first few weeks as châtelaine of the Manoir. It was all so new and so unexpected, yet she'd slipped into the role with far greater ease than she

would have believed possible a few weeks earlier. It was as if this new job had been waiting
for her all her life. She loved meeting the people on the estate, and learning about their problems. And they, instinctively sensing her gen-
uine interest, responded as they might not have
done had she not benefited from her experience in humanitarian work. It all seemed to
make sense now, she realized. Often she'd
asked herself what the purpose of her job in
Africa truly was, apart from the obvious. Now
it was plain to her. As though a bigger plan
had been underway, preparing her for the task
up ahead.

Glancing at the time, Natasha realized it was
getting on and that she was hungry. Henri and
his wife Mathilde were off this evening, so,
leaving the remote control next to the sofa,
Natasha made her way through the hall and
into the immense, old-fashioned kitchen to fix
herself a sandwich, having refused *madame*'s
offer of a meal left in the oven. She needed to
retain something of her former independence,
she realized ruefully, even if it was only making a sandwich on her own and not having it
presented on a silver platter.

But as she spread butter onto a crispy baguette she thought she heard a noise. Her head flew up and she listened carefully. It was easy to imagine hearing things in an old mansion like this one. After listening carefully, and realizing she must be mistaken, Natasha finished preparing her meal, added a glass of chocolate milk to the tray and headed back towards the *petit salon*.

It was then, as she was crossing the hall, that she caught sight of a shadow in the doorway. Her heart missed a beat and she nearly dropped the tray. Stopping dead in her tracks, she stared astonished at the outline of a young woman in eighteenth-century dress, her hair done up in ringlets, the expression on her face sad. Then, as quickly as it had appeared, the image faded, leaving her wondering if she'd imagined it. Quickly turning on the three-tier chandelier lights, she stared about the hall. But there was no vestige of the woman she could have sworn had stood there only instants earlier.

She must be dreaming, she decided, moving back into the salon and sitting down on the sofa. Still, the feeling lingered. And later, as she wandered up the main stairway on her way to bed, she stopped before Natasha de Saugure's portrait and shivered.

She'd be willing to swear the shadow she'd seen was the woman in the picture.

CHAPTER EIGHT

SATURDAY dawned reasonably fair, with a scattering of cloud. The Morrieux had insisted Natasha join them for dinner at Le Cercle, an exclusive club situated on the front at Deauville where, every year, a dinner was given to celebrate the end of the season's races, and a mock Battle of Waterloo was re-enacted between the British and French guests. As far as she could gather it was all very aristocratic, and to be a member you had to be able to trace your ancestry back over several generations.

Amused by the entire concept, Natasha had agreed to attend, and, as she didn't want to drive home late after having a drink, had booked herself into a room at the Normandy Hotel for the night, prepared to enjoy herself.

At seven o'clock the punctilious Philippe was waiting for her in the crowded lobby of the hotel, and together they walked the few hundred yards along the seafront to Le Cercle, where they were to meet the Comte and Comtesse and their friends for dinner.

But as they entered Natasha was amazed to see that the charming old building was falling apart. She glanced up uneasily at the cracked plaster in the ceiling, hoping it wouldn't collapse on top of her. The place was, in fact, as stately and yet as decrepit as the appearance of some of its ancient members, rigged out in black tie. But there was also an elegance and old-world nostalgia here, and as she observed all the Légions d'Honneur and Croix de Guerre sewn into the buttonholes of many of the more elderly members' lapels she was reminded of just how brave and gallant so many of these gentlemen were. They represented the courageous generation who'd fought in World War II—the reason why, today, people like herself were free to live in a democratic Europe.

As they entered the bar, and she shook hands with her hosts, Natasha was touched by this maintaining of old customs fast being replaced by other less gratifying practices.

Soon she was sipping a glass of champagne and conversing with the Comte de Morrieux, who was thrilled to learn of her interest in the history of their region. Then, when she least expected it, a familiar voice spoke at her side.

'Good evening, *mademoiselle*.' Raoul executed a small bow before he nodded to the Comte and Philippe hovering close by.

'Good evening,' Natasha murmured, trying not to appear flustered, livid that her pulse was fluttering once more. Surely she could be more controlled than this?

'So. You are being initiated into the customs of our society, I see.' His tone barely hid the irony.

'Yes,' she replied blithely, temper coming to her rescue. 'Philippe very kindly asked me to join him and his family here tonight, and tomorrow at the races. So kind,' she added, twirling around and bestowing a dazzling smile on the dumbstruck Philippe.

'Well, well. You must be the most envied man in the room tonight, Philippe,' Raoul murmured, his lips twisting in a thin sardonic smile.

'Uh, yes, of course. I am very happy to accompany Mademoiselle de Saugure—I mean Natasha.' He blushed, straightened his bow tie and tried not to let Raoul fluster him. It was always so. Raoul would walk in and take the floor. But at least tonight, Philippe reflected with a touch of pride, he'd made it to the winning post first and invited Natasha before any of his contemporaries had the chance.

Raoul was now complimenting the beaky-nosed Comtesse de Morrieux on her appearance, and Natasha noticed crossly that she was, of course, wreathed in smiles. 'I have asked Raoul to join us at our table,' she told her husband, who nodded approvingly.

'Very good, *mon vieux*, we don't see enough of you around here any more now that you spend so much time in Paris.'

Raoul threw Natasha a triumphant glance, read her annoyance at the invitation and felt a rush of satisfaction. So she was trying to set herself up in her own fashion in the region, was she? Had Philippe de Morrieux dangling after her too, did she? Well, he'd make short shrift of that little plan, he reflected, offering his arm to the Comtesse as they prepared to enter the dining room.

'Have you told Natasha about the Battle of Waterloo?' he enquired of Philippe, once they were all installed at table.

'Yes, after a fashion.'

'You'll enjoy that,' Raoul said, smiling benignly at Natasha. 'We have two teams, the English against the French. As you can see there are many of your compatriots here to-night—racing adepts, trainers. And then the big sales begin tomorrow, right after the last race. Many are here to acquire horses.'

'Fascinating,' Natasha murmured, turning her attention back to Philippe, determined not to give Raoul any quarter, while she desperately blinked away the images of their past encounter and tried to eclipse the physical sensation that just seeing him caused. She felt her nipples go taut under her evening dress and a troubling awareness haunted her. It was as though, when his eyes flew over her in that dark, possessive, disturbing manner, he were undressing her, stripping her of the protective sheath of silk and baring her for his pleasure.

She tried to pay attention to Philippe's stilted conversation. Surely Raoul couldn't tell how she was feeling? But when she took a fleeting sidelong glance in his direction and he smiled knowingly at her, she felt her cheeks burn with embarrassment.

He knew, damn him.

Of course he knew.

He had this whole game down to an art, knew exactly what he made a woman feel.

Taking a deep breath, and a few rather larger gulps of champagne than she'd intended, Natasha donned a glittering smile and continued to converse with the other members of the table. By the time the *ragout de Homard* was eaten and dessert served she was wilting under the strain, and sincerely wishing that she'd stayed at home and not exposed herself. Of all people the last person she would have imagined here tonight was Raoul, she thought as they sipped coffee. Yet deep down she knew that wasn't strictly true. Had she, in fact, come here secretly hoping that she would see him?

The thought sent another shudder and another rush of intimate sensations tingling through her pelvis. Damn Raoul. Why couldn't he just get up and leave instead of sitting there talking in that deep seductive voice, bringing her into the conversation whenever he could and being generally odious under the pretended solicitude?

Soon they were rising from the table and entering the room next door, where the Battle of Waterloo was already being prepared.

'We have another lady for the English team,' Raoul called out to the organizer, a short, busy Frenchman whom the others referred to as '*le général*'.

'Oh, no, please, I'd much rather watch,' Natasha said quickly. She had no desire to participate.

'What? You shrink from playing for your country? Come, come, Natasha, I thought better of you than this.'

'Please, Raoul, just leave me alone,' she muttered.

But Philippe was at her elbow now, leading her across the room towards the general. She looked back at Raoul, who was standing with his arms crossed and a broad grin on his face. He shrugged, letting her know he had no intention of saving her from her fate.

With a sigh, Natasha joined the other English ladies preparing to participate in the game. This really wasn't her thing. But what could she do? Without appearing disagreeable it would be hard to refuse.

'So, *mademoiselle*, here is a glass of champagne.' The general handed her a glass. 'You must drink it *à cul sec*—that means in one go—and then place the glass on your head. Then the next lady in line will do the same. Come on, try it. The team that finishes quickest wins. Now, try.'

'In one go?' Natasha queried, glancing uneasily at the glass.

'Yes. Have a go.'

'Okay.' Taking a deep breath, Natasha threw back the glass of champagne, spluttering as the liquid rushed into her mouth.

'Very good, very good.' The general smiled approvingly and refilled her glass. 'Now, ready to begin, everyone?

The two teams stood in line, side by side, and a good atmosphere reigned. The champagne, downed so quickly, was beginning to take effect, and Natasha felt somewhat lightheaded. When it came to her turn she tried to down the next glass under the encouragement of her team mates and ended up spluttering her way to the end and placing the glass on her head. She was positively dizzy now, and wished she could get away.

Then all at once Raoul was at her side, holding her elbow, steering her away. Somewhere in the surrounding haze she realized she'd said goodbye to the Comte and Comtesse and Philippe, and that she was being walked along the pavement held up by Raoul's strong arm.

'Why did you make me do that?' she asked, trying not to stumble.

'Careful, *ma belle*, you're not too steady on your pins. Lean on my arm. There, that's better.'

'Raoul, I don't think that was fair. You should have stopped them. I'm not used to all that champagne.' She gulped and hiccupped, and he laughed.

'Never mind. I'll give you a couple of Alka Seltzers back at the hotel, and after a good sleep you'll feel fine.'

'God,' she groaned, 'I don't want to think of what I'll feel like tomorrow morning.'

'You'll be fine. I guarantee it. Now, here we are at the Normandy. I'll take you to your suite. Have you got the key?'

She fumbled in her evening purse as they went to the lift and handed it to him while her head dropped on his shoulder. It felt so nice to lie against him; the scent of his aftershave smelled good. She felt his arm close firmly around her shoulders as they exited the elevator and made their way along the wide corridor to her suite.

Soon they were inside and Raoul closed the door behind them. 'Now, come and lie down,' he ordered.

'I don't want to lie down. I feel much better now,' Natasha said, giggling.

'Natasha, you've had a lot of champagne. I think it's better you rest.'

'Rest? I don't want to rest. Let's go out and dance. Let's have some more champagne.' She leaned against him and lifted her lips for his kiss. When it didn't come she made a moue and frowned. 'Don't you want to k-kiss me?' She gulped. 'I thought you seemed rather keen on it the other night.'

'You are not in a state to be kissed,' he answered firmly, taking her arm and leading her to the bedroom.

'That's not fair,' she said, shaking her head as she collapsed onto the bed, pouting. 'When *you* want to it's okay, but when I want...' Her voice trailed off and her eyes closed.

Raoul looked down at her and smiled. He shouldn't have put her forward for the game. It had been unfair of him and he knew it. In a quick, matter-of-fact manner he set about undressing her and slipped a nightgown over her head. As he was doing so Natasha's eyes opened. She smiled beatifically at him, then slipped her arms around his neck, pulling him down onto the bed.

'Natasha, this is not a good idea,' he muttered, trying to keep his physical reaction in check.

'Yes, it is,' she slurred, taking his hand and placing it on her breast. 'Mmmm. That feels so nice,' she mumbled as, unable to resist, he grazed her nipple.

'Natasha, you'll regret this in the morning,' he told her, trying to withstand the temptation of her lovely body while letting his other hand slip between her thighs. He was jolted by how wet and wanting she was.

But, instead of protesting, all Natasha did was sigh and surrender to his caresses. Raoul was tempted to undress and take her here and now. But something stopped him. An innate sense of honour. This would be tantamount to rape. He doubted he'd ever exercised such will-power, but exercise it he would. Instead of taking his pleasure he caressed her gently, his fingers penetrating her, following the writhing of her body as she arched up to him, pleading for more, then sighing when she came, before falling prostrate among the pillows, where she immediately fell into a deep and exhausted sleep.

Raoul rose, straightened his clothes and, after taking a long breath, tucked Natasha in. As he left the room he wondered what on earth had got in to him. With a shrug he returned to his own suite, and after a large brandy got ready for bed. He really must bed Natasha or get her out of his system once and for all, he decided firmly as he switched the light off.

One thing was for sure. He couldn't play this game much longer.

CHAPTER NINE

HAD she been dreaming or had Raoul carried her into the room last night and laid her on the bed? And had the rest of what she vaguely remembered been a figment of her fertile imagination, or had he once again made her feel the most incredible sensations she'd ever experienced?

Rubbing her eyes and letting out a long yawn, Natasha sat up and glanced at her watch. My God, it was almost eleven-thirty, and she was due to meet the Morrieux for drinks in the courtyard at twelve-fifteen.

As she entered the bathroom everything came back to her in quick succession, and a wave of embarrassment encompassed her. She really had Raoul to thank for removing her so promptly and efficiently from the scene. All she could hope for was that the Morrieux had not realized how tipsy she'd become after knocking back several glasses of champagne.

The mere thought of the stuff made her grimace. No more of that, she decided firmly, allowing the hot shower spray to soothe her tired body. And what about Raoul? she wondered, her thoughts lingering as she soaped herself. Where was he and what had prompted him to be so nice to her? It was really rather decent of him to have acted as he had. And, she realized ruefully, as her memory jolted, not to have taken advantage of her weakness and vulnerability.

Again her cheeks flamed at the thought of her wanton behaviour of the night before. She had practically—no, she *had*, let's be honest—invited him to make love to her.

As she wrapped herself in a large white terry towel, Natasha realized that there was little she could do except try and carry things off with as much dignity as possible. Though, knowing Raoul as she was beginning to, she doubted he would forego any chance of reminding her.

But there she was wrong.

Several hours later, when their paths crossed at the races, Raoul gave no knowing sign of recollection. In fact, he was very punctilious. And, as Natasha squirmed for several uneasy minutes, he simply made light conversation with the Morrieux, gave the Comte a tip on the horse he considered would win the next race, and asked her if she'd like to back the horse too.

After a while, she felt easier, and was able to enjoy the elegant, amusing atmosphere of the racecourse. Several ladies were dressed to the nines, others like herself, were discreetly elegant. All in all, she reflected, it had—apart from last night's embarrassing interlude—been a very agreeable stay-over. And even the interlude, she reflected ruefully, had been delicious.

Giving herself a quick jolt, Natasha refused to allow her mind to linger on Raoul's fingers gently caressing her. But all too often during the afternoon his kisses and his caresses coloured her thoughts. She would look at him from afar, unable to deny how very male and handsome he was, how devastatingly attractive. She couldn't prevent herself from experiencing a rush of something akin to jealousy when she saw him deep in conversation with a pretty and very chic blonde woman.

This simply must stop, she protested silently, turning her head and entering into an animated conversation with the staid Philippe, who was only too enchanted to be taken notice of by his lovely new neighbour. His parents looked on approvingly. A match between the Morrieux heir and the heir to the Saugure properties would be no mean feat.

The proximity of the two young people had not gone unnoticed by another member of the local community. All the while he was carrying on a flirtatious conversation with his cousin, Raoul had one eye on Natasha. Philippe de Morrieux—a rival! Why, the notion was laughable. Yet she did seem very open to being courted by that young man. A rush of anger overcame him. The little flirt had been writhing in his arms only a few hours ago. Was he perhaps wrong about her character? What sort of game was she playing?

He considered the thought as he approached the betting window and placed a solid bet on an outsider in the upcoming race. He glanced back at her and his lips twisted into a smile before he glanced once more at the list, then made another bet. Then slowly he approached the table in the paddock restaurant, where Natasha was seated with the Morrieux. The Comte welcomed him and told him to sit down.

'I can't, I'm afraid. I'm off to see the next race.'

'Did your horse win?' Philippe asked.

'I'm afraid not. It came in third, though, which wasn't too bad. By the way, I placed a bet for you in the next race,' he said, casually addressing Natasha. 'Would you like to come with me to the box and see if we are in luck?'

She hesitated. His eyes were boring into hers with a determination that was hard to resist. She glanced at the Comtesse, who was engaged in conversation with another elegant, bejewelled older lady.

'Why not?' she said with a shrug and a smile. 'Philippe, will you come too?'

'Oh? Yes, yes, of course—*avec plaisir*.' He grinned broadly and jumped up from his chair, ready to escort Natasha.

This was not the way he'd planned matters, and the presence of this innocuous young man annoyed Raoul profoundly. But there was nothing for it but to put a good face on it, so he smiled, and together the three of them walked across the paddock and over towards the building where Raoul had his box.

Soon they were watching the horses move towards the starting gates.

'See the jockey with the blue and white shirt over there?' he said, pointing.

'Yes.'

'That's our man.'

'What's the name of the horse?' she asked, eyeing the program.

'*I Want You.*'

'Excuse me?' She looked up and their eyes met.

'You asked me the horse's name.'

'Yes, I did.'

'Well, that's it. The horse is called *I Want You.*'

'Oh, I see.' She looked away, flustered, her colour rising once more, for the look in his eyes told her there was a not-so-subtle *double entendre* to his words that had nothing to do with the race.

'Maybe we'll get lucky,' Raoul added, glancing at her wickedly before lifting his racing glasses. 'Here, take these. You'll see the race better.'

'Thank you.' She accepted the glasses, glad of an excuse to have something to do other than feel his eyes upon her.

Philippe was studiously reading the programme, and began weighing up the pros and cons of several animals with Raoul. Placing the two men side by side was really rather unfair, Natasha realized ruefully, a spark of humour flashing. Raoul might not have been pleased that she'd asked him to join them, but in reality he should be happy if what he wanted was to promote himself. Next to the stiff, pasty Philippe, he shone like a diamond of the first degree.

Then the race began and all eyes focused on the galloping horses making their way along the straight. Natasha watched through the glasses, excited. She'd never had a bet on a horse before. Now she peered keenly, excitement mounting as *I Want You* edged to the forefront of the race. The crowd rose from their seats, crying encouragement. When in the last few seconds *I Want You* tore ahead by a length to win the race, Natasha was as excited as the rest.

'He did it!' She turned excitedly to Raoul. 'Isn't that wonderful? I can't believe he won. How clever of you to bet on him.'

'It was obvious that he had to win,' Raoul replied with a mischievous grin.

'Really? I thought you said he was an outsider with twenty to one odds.'

'He was.'

'So?' She raised her brow, truly curious as to the reason he'd been so sure. 'How were you so sure he'd win?'

'Because I want you,' he whispered in a lowered voice, his hand slipping over hers and squeezing it in an imperceptible yet intimate gesture.

Confused, Natasha drew away. It was all happening too quickly. She was so attracted to Raoul, yet she sensed the danger she would get into should she surrender to her desire for him. He was so sophisticated and worldly, and once more Clothilde's words of warning rang in her ears.

'I'm going back to my place after collecting our winnings,' he remarked in a very different tone, as though he hadn't noticed that she'd not answered.

'Ah, yes. Well, I must be getting back, too.'

'Why don't you come by and have a drink? Or rather, upon reflection, why don't we stop off for dinner somewhere? There is a very lovely little restaurant in Beaumont that you simply must discover.'

'Raoul, I need to get back, I have my car waiting, I—'

'Just a moment,' he instructed, lifting his index finger authoritatively. He pulled out his mobile and before she could stop him was making arrangements to have her car delivered back to the Manoir.

'Raoul, I never said I was coming with you,' she protested, exasperated. The man was far too sure of himself, she concluded, wishing she had the strength to refuse him point-blank, but knowing instead that she had every intention of going.

The restaurant turned out to be as charming as he'd predicted, with low beams and dried flowers, pristine tablecloths and attentive service. The food was undeniably delicious, and his company, she admitted reluctantly, was delightful.

Raoul went out of his way to put her at ease and to make her feel good in his company. He didn't quite understand why he was bothering to go to all this effort, though being pleasant to women came naturally to him. Still, something in Natasha compelled him.

'Raoul, I want to ask you a question.' She laid her forearms on the table and clasped her hands.

'Go right ahead, *ma chère*,' he invited, taking a sip of the excellent claret he'd ordered.

'It's about your ancestor, Regis d'Argentan. What exactly happened to him and Natasha? Why is everyone so secretive about them?'

The raised glass poised in mid-air. 'Why are you so curious about the past?' he asked, swirling the wine.

'Because it fascinates me. I want to know all about the history of the place. After all, I've decided to make it my home. I know that Natasha de Saugure and Regis were in some way connected.' She hesitated, then decided to tell him. 'You know, a funny thing happened the other night.' She glanced at him, swallowed, wondered if she should divulge her experience.

'Go on,' he urged, looking at her eyes narrowed. 'What happened?' He laid his glass down, giving her his full attention.

'Well, you'll probably think I'm mad, but I could have sworn that I saw her, standing in the doorway of the salon.'

'Saw who?' His brows met in a thick ridge above his patrician nose.

'Natasha de Saugure. I—well, this all sounds so silly, but—' She raised her hands and looked embarrassed.

'There is nothing silly about seeing a ghost,' he remarked, as though it were an everyday occurrence.

'You mean, you think it actually could be her?'

'Why not? It is not uncommon for strange things to be seen in ancient *demeures*. Whether they are real or not can be debated. But there are those who claim to have seen them.'

'Have you seen ghosts at your castle?' she enquired, brows shooting up.

'I wouldn't go so far as to put it in the plural.' He laughed. 'But there have apparently been sightings at certain times. Not that I give much credibility to such stories,' he added, eyeing her again, as though he were about to say more but then thought better of it.

'Raoul, do tell me—please.' She reached her hand across the table and placed it on his forearm. Raoul looked down, felt his arm tingle at the touch of her fingers, and restrained a sudden urge to take the hand in his and hold it.

'It all happened a long time ago,' he said reluctantly as she removed her fingers. 'Regis was a young man at the start of the French Revolution. He fought for the *aristos* and got himself involved in complicated doings.'

'Oh? Such as?'

'He was not wise in his choice of friends,' Raoul answered shortly. 'Now, shall we choose dessert? The strawberries should be excellent at this time of year.'

'Raoul, please don't fob me off. I want to know.'

'I'm sure Monsieur le Curé can give you a better and more balanced account of the past than I.'

'But why? It's just a story of something that happened over two centuries ago. Surely it's not that important?'

'Apparently important enough for it to still haunt the present. You told me you believe you saw Natasha. How do you know it was her?'

'Because she looked the same as the girl in the portrait on the stairs. I'm certain.'

'You know why Natasha was called Natasha?' he asked, changing the subject subtly.

'No, actually, I don't. I didn't even know it was a family name until I came here. My father never mentioned it. I just thought my parents liked the name.'

'Natasha's mother came from a noble Russian family. That is why she named her daughter thus.'

'And Regis fell in love with her?' She looked him straight in the eye.

'Yes,' he said slowly. 'Regis fell in love with her.'

'But?'

'How do you know there was a ''but''?' he queried.

'Because of the way you said it. Because in the family book of the Argentans she appears as nothing more than a hand-scribbled note in the margin. Not as his wife.'

'Natasha played fast and loose with him,' he retorted sharply. 'She played with his feelings and his safety. It was a difficult and dangerous time. He took extraordinary risks for her sake and she—well, she did something unforgivable.'

'I see. So the family never got over their hurt pride.'

'That is ridiculous,' he scoffed, snapping the menu shut. 'Hurt pride, indeed. We are talking of honour, *mademoiselle*. Natasha had no honour. She pledged her word to Regis and then flew into the arms of a revolutionary.'

'I see.'

'No, you don't. Few people today understand those times. She prostituted herself with a traitor.'

'Was there a reason for her action? Didn't she love Regis?'

'So she claimed,' he said witheringly. 'But she was all too happy to spread her legs for the local revolutionary leader. It caused a rift between the Argentans and the Saugures for several generations. But thankfully that is all in the past, and the two families maintain friendly relations once again.'

'I see.' Seeing the anger in his eyes, and the taut expression, Natasha realized she'd do better to change the subject. At least now that she knew a part of the story she could get the Curé to tell her more. 'I think strawberries would be an excellent choice,' she said, smiling winningly, glad to see his features relax.

'With cream?'

'Why not? Though I've eaten so much these past few days I must be putting on pounds.'

'You certainly don't look any heavier to me,' he responded, his eyes giving her a quick, all-encompassing scrutiny that left her swallowing and wondering how, in the flick of an instant, he could make her feel as though he'd undressed her. When his eyes rested a moment longer on her breasts she felt her nipples stiffen and ache longingly against her thin cotton bra. How could she be so brazen? How could this man leave her so vulnerable, so needy?

As though he could read her every thought, Raoul smiled and reached his hand across the table. 'Natasha, let me tell you something.'

'What's that?' she asked warily.

'To *want* is not a sin. It is a natural, healthy reaction. And don't pretend you don't know what I mean, because you do. Very well. Last night proved that to me.'

'Last night was—was an aberration,' she muttered, trying to resist the delicious sensation of his finger caressing the inside of her bare forearm in what was turning into a dangerously erotic motion.

'Last night was the proof that you want to make love with me,' he murmured huskily. 'In fact, I have already made love to you. Only not fully. The rest is still to come.'

'I—'

'Shush…' he ordered, slipping a finger over her lips. 'No more words. Just allow things to take their course. But, please, don't resist what we both know must occur between us.'

To her relief the waiter appeared with the strawberries and Raoul immediately returned to his former self. It was so hard to know what to do, she reflected, savouring the delectable fruit on her tongue, unaware of how sexy she looked as she bit into the fruit's red texture. Part of her admitted he was right. That sooner or later the fire must be consumed for it to burn out. Another part told her to take care, to beware, not to give in to him so easily, even though he knew perfectly well what her feelings were.

CHAPTER TEN

BY THE time they'd finished dinner and returned to the Ferrari it was dark. A near full moon lit the inky sky, illuminating the pretty Norman village with its hanging flower baskets, neat cobbled streets and crooked Tudor-style houses. She sighed. If anyone had told her a few weeks ago that she was going to be driving through a Norman village in a Ferrari, next to one of the handsomest men she'd ever met whose sexual advances she was finding it hard to resist, she would have laughed outright. Yet now the thought of spending a whole night in Raoul's arms enticed more than it frightened.

'There is somewhere I would like to show you before I take you home,' he said, taking a turning on the country road bordered by shadowy hedgerows.

'What's that?' she clasped her hands nervously.

'A place I think you may find intriguing.'
He kept his eyes on the road and said no more
until they'd turned off down a country lane, at
the end of which stood a small yet well-kept
cottage.

'What is this?' she asked, her heart missing
a beat.

'It is the cottage where Natasha and Regis
used to meet in secret in the days of the Terror
and after,' he replied quietly. 'It was here they
made love for the first time.'

Her head flew round and she looked at him,
not knowing what to say. It was obvious that
he'd brought her here for a reason. But why,
when he seemed so angry about these ancestors, would he want to bring her to the very
spot where they'd come together?

'I brought you here because I thought it
might be nice for you to see the cottage,' he
said, his tone non-committal as he got out of
the vehicle.

Two minutes later they were walking towards the front door. Raoul produced a large,
ancient, heavy-looking key and inserted it in
the lock. Soon the door creaked open.

'How come you have the key to this place?' she asked, stepping inside.

'Because I own it. It is part of the Argentan estate.' He switched on the light and Natasha looked about her, amazed at how little must have changed since the days when the two lovers had met here in secret.

'It must have looked just like this when they were here,' she whispered, allowing her fingers to trail over the ancient velvet settee.

'Yes, I believe very little has changed. My grandmother had the furniture re-upholstered, and some of the pieces restored. Also she had bathrooms and electricity installed. But come,' he said, reaching for her hand and leading her towards the stairs.

And suddenly she knew why they were here.

This was it, Natasha realized, overwhelmed by the significance of being in this place. Was it a trick? A way of getting her to submit to his desire for her? Or was there more to his sudden decision to bring her here?

As they climbed the ancient crooked stairs Natasha's pulse leapt and her skin tingled with anticipation. When they reached the door of the bedroom and he opened it she hesitated.

'This is where they made love,' he said quietly, drawing her inside, 'and this is where I shall make love to you,' he murmured, moving inside and lighting two candelabra perched on the stone mantel over the fireplace.

Natasha looked about her at the four-poster bed, draped in ancient tapestries, noting that it had been made up with fresh linen, as though awaiting them. There were flowers on the windowsill. The room glowed softly under the flickering flames of the candles and all she could do was imagine the two young people of long ago, entwined on that same bed.

But before her imagination could reach any further back in time Raoul was fixing her in the present. He moved across the room and placed his hands on her shoulders. Their eyes locked as though mesmerized, caught in the magic of the moment. When he began slowly unzipping her dress and unhooking her bra she made no protest, merely waited for his lips to touch hers, to feel what was fast becoming a familiar delicious exchange of sensations. Before the kiss was over, his tongue teasing expertly, her clothes were lying strewn about

her on the floor and she stood naked before him.

Drawing his head away, Raoul took a step
back and studied her. 'Beautiful,' he said, his
voice husky, 'Just as I knew you would be.
Come.'

Unable to do more than surrender to his
command, Natasha took his hand and allowed
him to lay her on the bed.

He was extraordinarily tender, not the fierce
lover she'd imagined, and as she lay among
the lavender-scented sheets all she could do
was close her eyes and feel, bask in the delight
of his ever more intimate caresses, feeling his
lips lightly graze the tips of her nipples, his
fingers slipping gently between her thighs, languorously discovering each tiny secret spot of
pleasure until she could bear it no more.
Arching towards him, Natasha let out a small
cry as at last he brought her to satisfaction.

Raoul gazed down at her, eyes gleaming.
She was wondrous, deliciously wondrous. But
he had only just begun.

In several quick movements he had divested
himself of his clothes and was lying next to
her, naked. She had no experience of men, he

realized as his hands resumed their wander-
ings, and to his surprise he discovered that he
liked it that way. Part of her was hesitant and
stiff, and he sensed there must be a story behind it. All at once he felt angry with whoever
the man was in her past, who'd made love to
her incompetently. But he would remedy that,
he vowed, reaching over and placing himself
above her.

'I am going to make love to you, *chérie*,' he
murmured, opening her thighs with his knee.
'Just lie back and enjoy it.'

Natasha could do no more than let out a
long sigh and obey. When she felt him thrust
firmly inside her a little gasp escaped her. Then
her muscles relaxed and she let him enter deep
inside, each thrust bringing him closer to her
core. Then, without realizing it, she picked up
his rhythm. Her hips arched and moved with
him as their bodies intertwined. Finally, when
neither could bear it any longer, they came together, hurtling over the edge, exploding with
pleasure before tumbling among the sheets and
lying saturated in each other's arms.

He had expected a pleasurable experience, but
nothing like this, Raoul reflected once he was

able to think straight. He had not made love to a woman like this in years, had not met with such reciprocated passion—ever.

The shock of the truth of this last statement hit him like an inside curve ball. *Mon Dieu*, this could become dangerous. Already was. He had never allowed anyone to reach into the confines of his heart. Not since Janine. Not since he'd suffered rejection. Once was quite enough, and he'd vowed at the early age of nineteen never to subject himself again to such raw humiliation.

But as he looked down at Natasha's sleeping form, her lovely golden mane strewn carelessly over the pillow, glistening in the moonlight, he felt something he hadn't thought he still possessed: a feeling of deep tenderness.

Quickly he rose from the bed and, slipping on an ancient silk dressing gown that hung behind the door, he moved towards the window, where he perched on the ledge. What had incited him to bring Natasha to this place? It had been a foolish decision, he realized in retrospect. For, although this night had been very near perfect, the spot held other connotations. Deep implications for both their families. And, since he had no intention of pursuing an affair with her, it was dangerous. Now he'd bedded her he must consider himself satisfied and be off to Paris first thing. There was no use hanging around and letting her believe he was prepared to get involved, for he wasn't. As he'd remarked several times, women had a disagreeable tendency to mistake a good night's sex for love. And he'd be willing to bet that Natasha was no exception.

He sighed. Why did it have to be like this? Why couldn't it all be simple? He would love to have another few nights like this, with no strings attached. But he had the nasty feeling that wasn't going to be possible.

Just then Natasha opened her eyes sleepily and stretched. So it had finally happened. She had let Raoul make love to her. All at once she came to, and realized she was alone in the bed. Fully awake now, she let her eyes wander across the room and she saw him, silhouetted in the moonlight. She experienced a wave of tenderness. How wonderful it had been, how simple and unimaginably perfect.

Natasha's eyes rested on Raoul and her pulse beat faster. He had made love to her, here in the very bed where their ancestors had joined, in this nest of forbidden passion. But common sense prevailed and she quickly told herself not to set too much store by this. She'd had a feeling Raoul might use whatever lures he thought necessary to break down her resistance.

And he had.

She had fallen for the bait, if bait it had been. Perhaps she was being cynical. Perhaps for now she would let herself believe that he too had sensed the shadow of the past hovering over them, and that something inexplicable had compelled him to bring her here rather than just lust.

Slipping from the bed, Natasha tiptoed across the ancient wooden floor. 'Awake?' she whispered.

Raoul turned, startled by her unexpected approach.

'I'm enjoying the night,' he said, slipping an arm about her and drawing her close. 'Look at that moon. It shines so clear and so bright.'

'I wonder if they ever had a night like this,' she murmured.

'You mean Regis and Natasha?' he queried, stiffening.

'No. I meant the local cats, Raoul. You know perfectly well I meant our ancestors. And I don't know why you're so loath to talk about them. After all, you're the one who brought me here,' she added, cross with him for pretending to misunderstand.

'I know. And I have been regretting it for the past half-hour. It was a silly notion.'

A stab of hot pain pierced her soul.

So she'd been right. It had been nothing but a clever ploy, a manner in which to pierce her shield and reach her at her most vulnerable. Swallowing the lump in her throat, she moved from the curve of his arm.

'I think we'd better get back. I have a lot to do tomorrow,' she muttered in as firm a voice as she could muster. It was hard to swallow, hard to think, hard to hold back the tears burning her eyes. But she was determined that Raoul wouldn't see how deeply the experience had affected her. Let him think that, like him, she had merely taken pleasure in an enjoyable bout of sex and now she was ready to move on.

'Very well,' he answered, lifting his brows. A strange feeling of emptiness gripped him as he watched her move towards the bathroom— a modern addition his grandmother had insisted on. He hadn't expected her to react quite like this. Perhaps he'd been too brusque. But he didn't want to get into a whole diatribe about Regis and the former Natasha. Particularly now that he'd decided to cool things down a tad.

Hadn't he?

Raoul swung off the windowsill and stood a moment in the darkness. Then with an impatient gesture he grabbed his clothes from the floor and began to dress. He couldn't analyze all this right now. He would think about it some time tomorrow. If at all. The best thing was exactly what was occurring. And the sooner he dropped Natasha at home the better it would be for both of them.

Half an hour later they were driving in silence through the cool Normandy night. Soon they had reached the gates of the Manoir and were rolling up the drive.

It was five in the morning, Natasha realized, suddenly embarrassed at what Henri and the servants might think of her appearing home in the middle of the night with Raoul. But, after all, they'd been away, which made it simpler to explain.

When the car rolled up to the front door, she summoned up her courage and prepared to bid him a cool, disinterested goodbye, but was impeded from saying it when he slipped from the car and took her case out of the back. Reluctantly Natasha followed suit and exited the vehicle.

'Thank you for a very pleasant dinner,' she said coolly as he deposited the case on the large stone step.

'You're very welcome,' he answered, eyeing her closely as she fiddled in her bag for her key. Soon it was inserted in the lock and she turned it.

This was it, Natasha realized, gathering all her dignity. 'Well, goodnight, Raoul. I'm sure I'll see you around some time. Our paths will inevitably cross, I imagine.'

'Natasha—' He cut himself short, taken aback by her coolness, the way she was brushing him off. It was unheard of. Nobody brushed off the Baron d'Argentan in this off-hand manner.

'Goodnight,' she said again brightly, picking up her case and standing with her hand on the door, clearly meaning to close it.

'Goodnight,' he muttered finally, unable to decide whether to kiss her or not. As the door closed firmly on him Raoul swore under his breath. Never, in the course of his active life, had any woman closed the door in his face. Except in a flaming row. But that was different, he reflected, gunning the engine and heading off angrily down the drive. Flying crockery and slamming doors were fine when you were in the middle of a passionate row that would likely end up horizontally.

But this… This was unheard of.

Grinding his teeth, he swerved onto the country road, barely missing a milk van.

He would teach Natasha a lesson, he vowed. Damned if he would take her impertinence lying down.

Leaning back against the front door, Natasha let her head drop and sighed shakily. It had taken all her courage to act the way she had.

But there was no doubt inside her that it was for the best. Raoul was history. And although part of her regretted tonight's tryst—for that was what it had been, if truth be told—at least she'd know what it was like to feel truly wonderful in a man's arms.

But at what cost? she wondered, picking her case up and making her way silently up the large staircase. When she reached Natasha's portrait she stopped for a moment and peered up at her in the half-light. Had she too experienced similar sensations in the arms of Raoul's ancestor? And what had happened to make Raoul so loath to talk about them? For a moment she lingered, then proceeded on to her bedroom. She simply must unravel the mystery, find out why Raoul felt so strongly about her ancestor. Something very serious must have happened for it still to affect someone of his generation.

Tomorrow, she vowed, undressing, her fingers smoothing her skin softly, recalling his touch and the scent of him, she would call the Curé and try to discover more.

But for now she must try, despite her pain and her agitation, to get some sleep.

CHAPTER ELEVEN

'*MADEMOISELLE*, you have a visitor,' Henri announced as she sat, several days later, going through the household accounts.

'Oh? Right. Who is it?' She brushed her hand through her hair and wondered why the numbers never tallied. Arithmetic wasn't her best subject.

'It is Monsieur le Maire,' Henri said proudly. 'He was away on holiday all this time, visiting his relations in America. But now he has returned and has come to pay his respects.'

'Good. Well, show him into the *salon*,' she said with a smile, aware that another morning was blown. Not that she really cared. In fact, quite the opposite. Lately it had been hard to concentrate on her duties, and any excuse to avoid them was welcome.

She glanced in the mirror. It was impossible to hide the wan look on her face, however hard she tried. Eating had been somewhat difficult of late. And she couldn't help her pulse leaping every time the phone rang.

Just in case it was Raoul.

But of course it never was.

It was over, and the sooner she got the message the better.

Moving across the hall, Natasha entered the *salon*, surprised to see a young, handsome Frenchman standing before her wearing corduroys, a cashmere jersey and a blazer. She'd expected someone bald and middle-aged.

'Mademoiselle de Saugure—what a pleasure. I'm so sorry I was absent all this time. May I present myself? Gaston Mallard at your service.' He bowed over her hand, then smiled a handsome open smile that Natasha immediately took to.

'It's a pleasure to meet you too,' she said, smiling back and inviting him to sit down. 'Would you like some coffee? Or something stronger, perhaps?' She glanced at her watch. It was almost midday. 'I think we could allow ourselves a glass of wine, don't you?'

'I would be delighted.'

'Then, Henri, please bring some white wine.'

'Très bien, mademoiselle.' Henri closed the door discreetly behind him while Natasha took the opportunity of studying her guest more closely. He was extremely good-looking, with chestnut hair and blue eyes, of medium height and well dressed. Most of all there was something frank and inviting about him. To Natasha, living in the aftermath of her unfortunate night with Raoul, he came as a breath of fresh air.

'So, you've been *maire* of the village for a while?' she asked, sitting opposite him.

'Two years. It was almost an inherited post,' he added, laughing. 'My father and grandfather were *maire* before me, back to the days of the Revolution, and so I suppose it was my turn to take over.' He laughed again and shrugged. 'I run a calvados business near here. We like to think that this old family tradition is very unique and that we make the best and oldest calvados in Normandy.'

'And do you?' she queried, her face breaking into a small laugh at his open demeanour.

'The truth?'

'Absolutely.'

'Well, I think we make excellent calvados, but whether it is the best or not I couldn't say.' He frowned jokingly. 'But you must vow on your life that if you come across my grandfather or father you will never say that. They would disinherit me in the same instant.'

'Goodness. I would hate for that to happen,' she exclaimed, laughing, relaxing for the first time in days.

By the time they'd had a glass of wine and chatted some more Natasha felt very pleased to have made a new friend. Gaston was charming, friendly, and surprisingly unflirtatious—which, coming from a Frenchman, was something.

'Why don't you stay for lunch?' she asked, on the spur of the moment.

'I would love to,' he responded regretfully, 'but unfortunately I have a committee meeting early this afternoon. But...' he hesitated.

'Yes?' she prompted.

'I was going to suggest that, should you like, we could dine together. Perhaps tomorrow night?'

'That would be very nice,' she agreed happily. This man's company would do her good, and help get Raoul out of her mind and system.

'Good. Then I shall pick you up around seven-forty-five tomorrow. There is a very nice little restaurant in Beaumont that I think—'

'Oh, no,' she cut in, before she could stop herself.

'You don't like Beaumont? You already know it?'

'Yes—no. What I mean is that perhaps it would be fun to try something else. I've already been to Beaumont.' She rescued herself hastily. 'I'd love to discover some of the other places around.'

'Very well.' Gaston opened his hands in a gesture of accord. 'Then I shall think of somewhere I am certain you have not visited previously. Goodbye, *mademoiselle*.' He lifted her hand gallantly to his lips.

'Please, call me Natasha. It makes me feel as if I'm a hundred when everyone treats me so formally.'

'*Très bien*, then Natasha it shall be. And you shall call me Gaston.'

They smiled in a friendly manner and Natasha accompanied him to the front door. What a charming man, she concluded, closing it after him. How nice that she'd met someone fun and engaging; someone, she reflected glumly, who could take her mind off Raoul's silence.

After a light lunch, determined not to fall into the dumps—a frequent occurrence of late—she stepped out into the garden, where André the gardener was busy clipping the hedge. She took a deep breath and lifted her face towards the sky, watching the fast-moving cloud, the patches of blue interspersed with grey announcing possible rain later in the day. Perhaps she should take a walk down to the village and pass by the Curé's house—a plan she'd promised herself to carry out but still hadn't found the time to execute.

Stepping back inside, Natasha picked up a jacket in the hall, that was fast becoming less formal than her grandmother would ever have deemed proper, and slipped outside. She began walking at a good pace towards the village, waving across a field at Rolland Hervier, one of the tenant farmers on her land, riding the knew combi-harvester that the estate had invested in. She liked seeing the people happy and busy, knowing that her actions were causing the place to become more productive. And she felt a deep sense of belonging.

As she stepped into the cobblestoned village street several people smiled and said hello. Madame Blanc from the bakery, Rémy from behind the bar at the café, Monsieur Lenoir at the *tabac*, who now ordered the English newspapers for her.

'A nice day, *mademoiselle*,' he commented as she stepped inside the small cluttered shop.

'Yes. It is. Did *The Times* arrive?'

'I'm afraid only yesterday's. It's all due to this silly new distribution system they've implemented. Everything comes from Paris now.' He shook his grey head disapprovingly. 'But one can't do anything about it, I'm afraid. It's the way of the world. Change. Always change.' He shook his head again. 'I was saying to my wife only the other night that we are really quite lucky. Not much here has changed. Though of course when the Baron gets married things will probably take a turn. The new Baroness will want things her own way, no doubt.' He sniffed, and Natasha swallowed.

'You mean the Baron d'Argentan?'

'Of course. When we refer to the Baron here we mean him. The Marquise de Longueville, who lives over in Falaise, has been spreading the news around. Apparently the Baron has become very attentive to her only daughter, Camille. Though between you and me I can't see what he sees in her,' he added, leaning conspiratorially across the chocolate bars.

'Well, I'm sure she's a very nice girl,' Natasha said weakly, trying to rid herself of a sudden dizziness that made her light-headed.

'No doubt. And it may all be a figment of the Marquise's imagination. She's been trying to fob that girl off on someone for the past ten years. Of course the Baron would be a great catch.' He nodded sagely. 'A great catch indeed.'

'I'm sure.' Natasha braced herself. 'Well, if the papers haven't arrived I'd better be on my way. Goodbye, Monsieur Lenoir, à bientôt.' Hastily she retired from the shop, glad to be outside once more, afraid her sudden rush of emotion might show. So she was right. He'd merely wanted to bed her to prove to himself that he could. Well, he'd done a pretty good job, she recognized bitterly as she hurried down the street, anxious not to get caught in another round of conversation she didn't feel up to. Her mind was in turmoil, and her heart felt a strange stab of hurt. Which was ridiculous, of course, since there was nothing between her and Raoul except a strong physical attraction.

'You look in a hurry.'

She spun around to see Gaston crossing the road to greet her. Mustering a smile, she responded.

'Hello, Gaston. How are you?'

'Fine.' He took his hand in hers and studied her closely. 'But you, *ma chère* Natasha, do not look so fine.' His brows met. 'Is something the matter?'

'No, no, I'm all right,' she protested, shocked that she could be so transparent. 'I just—' She stopped short, not knowing what to say.

'Why don't we have a coffee and a brandy?' he suggested in a comforting tone. 'And you can tell me—or not, as you wish—what is wrong. It must be quite lonely for you to find yourself in a new community. I can perhaps be a friend?' He raised a brow and smiled that warm, friendly smile she'd felt so drawn to at their meeting earlier in the day.

'Okay,' she said, smiling back. Together they walked back up the street to the café, where they settled at one of the small round tables on the pavement and Gaston ordered two *cafés filtres* and two brandies.

'Now. Will you consider me nosy if I ask what is troubling you? I barely know you, but friendship doesn't necessarily need time to develop.'

This last was true. Natasha had made many good friends on her African travels, some of them in little more than a moment.

'It's nothing. Just a piece of news that's left me a little off keel, that's all. But it's not important in the least.'

'You're certain? It didn't seem that way a few minutes ago. In fact, I felt you'd been hit over the head with a baseball bat, as the Americans say.'

'Not that bad.' She laughed, cheering up and feeling more her old self. 'Nothing to worry about.' She smiled, raised her brandy snifter, and they clinked glasses.

They chatted a while, and Gaston tactfully dropped the matter of what was ailing her. But just as they were finishing their drinks a familiar vehicle in the form of Raoul's black Range Rover drew up and parked on the opposite side of the street.

'Ah. There's Raoul. I think he was in Paris this past two weeks,' Gaston remarked, waving.

Natasha watched, heart sinking, as Raoul, dressed in jeans and a loose navy sweater, made his way lazily across the street. She felt her cheeks burn and her pulse jolt. Why did he have such an effect on her, damn it? Surely she could keep these feelings under control? It was ridiculous—shaming. The man had made it clear he wanted nothing more to do with her. Surely she'd got the message loud and clear?

Determined not to lower herself by showing any of these thoughts, Natasha plastered on a social smile.

'Gaston. Natasha. I see you two have met.' His eyes flashed over her. God, she was beautiful—though a little pale and flushed now that he looked closer. So Gaston had discovered the new local beauty. Well, well, well.

'Why don't you join us? We were just having *café* and cognac.'

'Good idea.' He drew up a chair and sat down between the two, his presence immediately dominating. 'So, you two are getting to know each other?'

Natasha caught the inflection behind the statement, the fleeting exchange between the two men, and wondered what was going on.

'Yes. I had the pleasure of meeting Natasha this morning. As you know, I've been away for a while and wasn't able to attend the funeral.'

Why did he need to justify his visit to the Manoir to Raoul? she wondered, annoyed at his high-handed air of owning the place. And there was Rémy, coming out solicitously from behind the bar to shake hands. She could have slapped Raoul at that moment for being so odiously larger than life.

'I think it's time I was going,' she remarked. She was damned if she was going to sit here being surveyed as though she were under a damn microscope. He'd made it plain he didn't want her, hadn't he? She pushed back her chair.

'So soon?' Raoul's brow rose and an amused smile hovered about his lips. Again the urge to slap him made her clench her fists into two tight balls.

'Actually, I have some things to do. Including stopping by Monsieur le Curé's,' she said sweetly. 'He's going to tell me some of the history of these parts. Like how our ancestors interacted. Things like that.' She sent him a bright, brittle smile and rose.

'I see. How about dinner tomorrow night?' he asked suddenly, his eyes boring into hers.

'That's very kind, but I'm otherwise engaged.' Natasha turned, flapping her eyelashes provocatively at the surprised Gaston. 'Thanks for the refreshment. And *à demain*.' She waved her fingers and, turning on her heel, made her way down the pavement, letting out a triumphant sigh of relief. *Serve you damn well right, Raoul d'Argentan.* That should put him in his place. At least now he'd know that he wasn't the last Coca Cola in the desert. That she'd been invited out by someone else. And someone not to be sneezed at. Gaston was handsome, self-assured, and he held a position of importance in the area.

With a determined nod she stepped past the church and moved towards the *cure*—the rectory—where she hoped to find the priest at home.

CHAPTER TWELVE

'SO YOU'VE met Natasha. What do you think of her?'

The question was delivered in a short, matter-of-fact manner that left Gaston in no doubt of Raoul's meaning.

'Yes, I have, and I like her,' he replied immediately, swirling his brandy thoughtfully and taking a quick oblique glance at his friend. Even though they came from very different backgrounds, Raoul and he had played together as boys, had been given a similar education, and had courted the village girls as they'd grown up. Even after Raoul had taken his place in Paris society and Gaston had remained in the village where he belonged, their friendship had flourished. 'Do I get the drift that you're interested in Mademoiselle de Saugure?' he threw out casually, taking a sip of brandy.

'Me? Interested? Why should I be interested in her? What an idea,' Raoul scoffed. 'I find her *sympathique*, at most. No.' He shook his head. 'I'm not interested in anybody right now.'

'Really? There's a rumour going about that you might ask for the Longueville girl's hand in marriage.' Gaston grimaced. 'Rather you than me, *mon vieux*.'

'What rubbish. I've known Camille all my life. God, I'd rather marry a jockey than marry her. All she can talk about is horses. Plus, she's hardly what I would think of as attractive. No, but I've been over there quite often lately, looking at some horseflesh.'

'Natasha is certainly attractive,' Gaston countered. 'And I'm glad to know you've no interest in that area.' He took a last swig and rose. 'Because I find her delightful. Really rather alluring. *Au revoir, mon ami. A bientôt.*'

Gaston nodded briefly, then turned on his heel and ambled up the street, a smile hovering as he made his way thoughtfully towards the Town Hall. Was his old friend Raoul more smitten than he cared to let on? Why, that would be something. Particularly in view of his family history. Of course it was to be hoped that if he did fall for Natasha the outcome would be more satisfactory than his ancestor's.

Gaston stopped a moment in the Plâce du Village. It was here, in the 1790s, where the guillotine had been erected on which his ancestor, Benoît, had nearly managed to have the Baron Regis d'Argentan beheaded. It always sent a weird sensation coursing through him to think of it. And it was the famous Natasha who had saved the two men from one another. He shook his head. What women did for the sake of a man they loved. And how stupidly men interpreted their actions, he reflected ruefully.

With a shrug and a sigh he turned and made his way into the Town Hall. All that was ancient history. Had nothing to do with today's world. Yet a funny feeling told him that history was repeating itself in a different manner.

But one which could prove just as fascinating.

Natasha paused at the door of the Rectory, then, lifting her right hand, banged the knocker several times.

Soon she heard shuffling footsteps in the corridor beyond and the door opened.

'Ah, *mon enfant*, it is you.' The old Curé, his white mane gleaming, beamed at her. 'Come in, come in, my dear. It is a pleasure to have you in my home.'

'Thank you so much. I hope I'm not disturbing you at a bad time?'

'Not at all. I was just trying to come up with an idea for Sunday's sermon. Perhaps you will inspire me.' He winked and smiled, and ushered her down a tiled corridor into a long beamed room that looked out over an attractive orchard.

'What a pretty room,' she remarked, gazing out of the window, enchanted. 'This is a very special house.'

'Yes, it is,' the Curé agreed, motioning to the sofa. 'Sit down, my dear, and let me order a cup of tea for us from Madame Sarasin.'

'Thank you.' Natasha didn't like to say that she'd just had coffee and cognac with the *maire*.

'So. You have come to discover more about your family. That is good. I'm glad to see what an interest you are taking in your inheritance. Such a shame that your father was unable to assume his duties as Comte. But we must not regret the past. It is God's will that things should have happened in this way.' He shrugged in a Gallic manner and came to sit opposite her. 'Now, tell me, my dear. What exactly would you like to know? There is so much—so many stories. Perhaps you should be specific.'

'Well.' Natasha clasped her hands, suddenly nervous. 'I wondered if you knew something of what happened to Regis d'Argentan and Natasha de Saugure, after whom I believe I must be named?'

The Curé's fingers steepled and he looked thoughtful. 'That is most interesting. And why, I wonder, would you be so intrigued by their story?'

'Oh, just general interest,' Natasha prevaricated.

'I see.'

Natasha got the feeling that this man saw a lot more than he made out, and she hastily continued, 'I am, of course, interested because of my name.'

'Why, naturally. And then you know Raoul. I heard you have been seen together dining, and at the races.'

A dull flush rose to her cheeks. 'Yes. Well—actually, we were. I went to the races with the Morrieux, but then—'

The Curé raised his hand in a peremptory gesture.

'You have no need to furnish me with any kind of explanation. It is not my business who you see or don't see. Raoul is a good young man, if somewhat lost. He suffered a bad experience in his youth, you know.'

'No, actually I didn't.'

'Yes, it was a shame. When he was nineteen he met a girl who played fast and loose with his heart and his hopes. Raoul was very fond of her. But she—well, she had a liking for adventure and wealth. She left him for an Arab sheikh. I don't think his pride has ever quite recovered.'

'I see.'

'I thought you would. Now, as for your Natasha—well, let me see. She began her career as any young aristocrat of her time would have. But that was cut short by the Revolution. They were terrible times that affected everyone's lives. Nothing would ever be quite the same again.'

'I can imagine that it must have been awful.'

'Yes. I believe it was. There were many rivalries settled in a dishonest fashion. Love affairs were avenged, jealousy and pain assuaged by the elimination of a rival.' The Curé folded his hands and sighed sadly.

'You mean that someone took revenge on Natasha?'

'Not on Natasha herself. But Benoît Mallard was in love with her. He knew she was out of his reach, she being an aristocrat and he a revolutionary. She'd been promised since childhood to Regis d'Argentan, with whom she was in love. But he was a flighty one. He had many mistresses and enjoyed life.'

'But weren't he and Natasha in love? I thought—'

'Yes. I believe that deep down they were. But they were two proud young people, caught up by events. Natasha didn't want to be one more notch on Regis's belt. And his wife, to boot. She knew Benoît loved her passionately. And frankly, from all I can gather, she encouraged him to believe that she would look favourably upon his suit simply to provoke Regis's wrath. Now, you can imagine how that must have affected the poor young man. Here he was, a simple merchant, with no hope of aspiring to the hand of such a wealthy noble lady as Natasha. And all of a sudden she lures him on, and the revolutionaries tell him that everyone is now equal.'

'Go on,' Natasha urged when he paused.

'Well, during the Revolution Mallard was given a position of power in the Nouveau Régime. It was too tempting not to use it. He had d'Argentan tried for treason, imprisoned, and sentenced to the guillotine.'

'So he was guillotined?'

'No. He escaped.'

'My goodness, how?' Natasha sat on the edge of her chair as history unwound before her.

'It was Natasha who saved him. But at a price.'

'What do you mean?'

'She slept with the enemy, so to speak.'

'You mean with Benoît?'

'Yes. Realizing that even now he still had no chance of marrying her, and that what would most hurt Regis would be to dishonour her, Benoît offered Natasha a pact: her virginity for Regis's life.'

'And she agreed?'

'Yes, she agreed.' The Curé nodded, raised his hands and sighed.

'And what happened?'

'Regis escaped with his head but never forgave her. He would have rather have lost it than see the woman he was promised to sullied by another. Particularly one he considered his enemy.'

'You mean he rejected her after all she'd done for him?'

'I'm sad to say that, yes, he did. Outwardly, that is. The two of them escaped to England together, but he refused to marry her, considering her a traitor to France and to the Royalist regime.'

'But that's absurd,' Natasha exclaimed angrily. 'She gave up what at that time was a most precious part of her life.'

'I know. But Regis was young and proud and stupid. He died an angry, bitter old man. Oh, they were able to return after the Revolution. Napoleon gave them back their lands and their castles. But they lived side by side for sixty years, married to other people without ever talking to one another again publicly.'

'Goodness, what a story.' Natasha swallowed and shook her head. No wonder the young girl in the portrait looked sad. She had given up everything for the man she loved and this was what she'd received in return. 'Was the Mallard in question Gaston Mallard's ancestor?'

'Yes. He was.'

'Yet Gaston and Raoul seem to be good friends.'

'Well, let us be thankful for the healing of time,' the Curé said benignly. 'After all, over two hundred years have elapsed since the events we speak of.'

'True. But tell me, there is a cottage I've heard about somewhere in the countryside where Natasha and Regis met.'

'Ah, so you've heard about that,' the Curé said, looking at her curiously. 'Not many people know that version of the story. I wonder— But, no—forgive me, that is none of my business.' He waved a hand. 'It is said that despite their public rejection of one another the lovers did in fact meet secretly in that cottage. It is on the Argentan estate, you know. The old Baroness, Raoul's grandmother, had things tidied up, but kept the original furnishings. It is said that the bed there is the same one the couple slept in. She apparently found the tale most romantic.'

'It is. Very.' Natasha swallowed. 'Well, I've taken enough of your time, *mon père*. I had better be on my way.'

'What? No tea?'

'No, thanks. Another time, with pleasure, but I think I'd better be getting back to the Manoir.'

'Very well.' The old gentleman rose and, taking her hand in his, held it a moment. 'You know, history need not necessarily repeat itself,' he murmured, in a low gentle tone. 'Raoul is a good man, despite his blindness. Maybe some day he will wake up.'

Then, before she could answer, he turned and conducted her back to the front door, and after a quick and warm goodbye Natasha was on her way.

CHAPTER THIRTEEN

IT WAS high time he returned to Paris, Raoul realized, staring in annoyance out of the mullioned window at the rain, pouring steadily as it had all day. But although he'd been tempted to get in the car, drive off and forget the whole matter, Raoul found himself incapable of blotting out the image of Natasha and Gaston cosily ensconced at the Café des Sports, chitchatting very comfortably.

And perhaps more.

It was this *perhaps more* that was the crux of the matter. He didn't mind her dining with his old pal, not in the least, he told himself repeatedly. But the idea that she might submit to his caresses as she had to his was infinitely more disturbing.

He glanced at his watch. Five o'clock. In a couple of hours Gaston would be picking Natasha up to drive her over to Honfleur for dinner. Or perhaps they'd changed plans since the weather was so rotten and were staying closer to home. Worse, maybe Gaston had invited her to dinner in his extremely charming low-beamed thatched farmhouse, which was, Raoul realized, eyes narrowing, an ideally romantic spot for seduction.

'Bon sang!' he exclaimed, bringing his fist down on the ancient stone parapet against which he'd been leaning. He would not allow this to happen—wouldn't let her slip through his fingers. He'd been a gentleman, hadn't he? Had not taken advantage of her inebriated state the other night, which he quite easily could have. Instead he'd respected her, waited for the right moment. Now she should jolly well respect him too. And anyway, what business did she have going to dine with another man? A man who, although he was his friend, was the descendant of one who had already sullied the family reputation. No, he decided, walking determinedly down the ancient worn steps to the Baronial Hall, he would not allow this to happen just like that.

Grabbing his Barbour jacket in the hall, Raoul banged the heavy front door behind him and, ducking from the rain, hurried to the Range Rover. It was time to take action.

Before things got out of hand, he reflected, gunning the engine.

Time to show her he meant business.

Curled up in the *petit salon*, Natasha was enjoying the end of a riveting novel which had helped take her mind off the images of Raoul that lingered, however determinedly she set them aside. It seemed that however hard she tried to banish him from her thoughts he kept creeping back in, the impression of his dark, windswept countenance hard to shake off. But the good news was that she was having dinner with Gaston, she reminded herself, laying the book down and staring into the flames. Gaston was charming and handsome, gallant and gracious. The perfect antidote to Raoul, who was arrogant, selfish, autocratic and odious.

Bracing herself, and for the hundredth time telling herself she was well rid of him, Natasha glanced at the ormolu clock on the mantelpiece. It was five-thirty. Soon she needed to go upstairs, have a bath with some of the delicious lavender bath essence she'd bought the other day in Deauville, and prepare for the evening's outing.

As she prepared to unfurl her long legs from under her Natasha heard the sound of a car in the drive. Who on earth could it be? Someone to see Henri, perhaps?

But her heart stood still when, stepping over to the window, she spied the familiar figure of Raoul getting out of the vehicle. Natasha swallowed and closed her eyes for a second. She should get Henri to say she wasn't at home. But as the doorbell clanged she knew she was not capable of doing that: the desire to see him, speak with him, feel him close was too tempting to resist.

'Stop it,' she admonished herself out loud. She was acting like a gooey teenager when she was a grown-up woman. Just because he was the first man to make her feel those wondrous sensations she'd experienced in his arms it didn't mean she was spineless.

Pulling herself together, Natasha marched out into the hall, determined to give him a set-down. Henri had already let him in and he was taking off his jacket.

'Ah. Natasha. I'm glad I found you at home. I have a problem I wish to discuss with you.' He sounded friendly and businesslike, and she wondered suddenly if she'd misread his sudden visit.

'Right. Well, I haven't much time.' She glanced pointedly at her watch. 'I have a dinner engagement.'

'This won't take very long. But I need to have your agreement,' he said, moving towards her and taking her hand in his.

Again the deadly tingling magic coursed up her arm and throughout her body. She swallowed and smiled coolly, despite her inner turmoil.

'We'd better go into the office,' she murmured, hoping that the austere atmosphere of this workspace would help her regain control.

'You mean you aren't going to offer me a drink on a filthy evening like this?' he cajoled, eyes meeting hers full-on.

'Uh, well, yes—of course. Henri, could you bring a bottle of wine to the *petit salon*, please?' she said, turning quickly and leading the way to the room she had just abandoned, hoping he couldn't read her mind, that the desire churning inside her was hers and hers alone to witness.

'Ah, it is good to be inside on such a miserable evening,' Raoul said, rubbing his hands and approaching the unlit fireplace. 'I hope Henri has seen to it that you have wood in for the winter. You'll need it. It gets quite chilly in these parts, and the central heating in this place isn't the most modern. Your grandmother refused to have a new unit installed. Said that anyone who was cold could damn well put on another sweater.' He rose and stood over her, eyes laughing. 'So, Natasha, *ma belle*, you look put out. Have I done something I shouldn't?'

'Not at all,' she dismissed coolly, perching on the arm of the sofa and crossing her legs protectively. 'But perhaps you'd like to state your business. I don't have much time.'

'Of course. But let's wait until Henri has brought the wine.'

'Very well. Do sit down,' she added formally, glad that her voice sounded chilly even to her own ears. 'How was Paris?'

'Fine, I imagine.' He shrugged and sat comfortably on the armchair opposite, slinging one corduroy-clad leg over the other while his arm rested elegantly over the back of the cushion.

He was too damn at ease, Natasha thought, quelling the images of him that night in the abandoned cottage, too damned at home for his own good. She simply had to put an end to these ridiculous fantasies.

A knock on the door announced Henri and the wine. Soon it was uncorked and Raoul was handing her a glass. When the door closed behind the manservant Natasha peered at Raoul over the rim of her glass.

'So. What brings you here this evening?' she asked frostily.

'Ah, yes, the reason for my visit. Well, you see, there is a fence that divides our properties on the southern boundary. There is some slight damage. I want to have it repaired but need your consent to do so.'

Natasha frowned. It sounded rather a weak excuse, and she wondered suddenly, her pulse picking up, if he'd come because he wanted to see her.

'I'm sure there isn't any problem. Is the fence my responsibility or yours?'

'Mine.'

'Then why would you need my permission to repair it?' she queried, her chin coming up.

'I really don't know why you bothered to come out on a rainy night to tell me this, Raoul. Surely our factors could have dealt with it?'

'*Bien sûr,*' he agreed smoothly. 'But as it is the first time that something has come up between the properties since you've become mistress, and because you left the other day in perhaps not the best of moods...' his brow rose and a smile twitched around his well-shaped lips '...I thought it would be more courteous to come personally.'

'Very thoughtful,' she answered dryly. She would not let him get the better of her. She could feel the tentacles of his influence reaching out, creeping around her, pulling her towards him in that mesmerizing manner she found so hard to resist. 'Well,' she continued, letting out a deep breath she'd been holding, 'that's fine. Do whatever has to be done. I really don't mind. But I'm afraid I'm going to have to ask you to leave soon. Gaston's picking me up in forty-five minutes.'

'So soon?'

'Yes.'

'I see. Well, let us finish this glass of wine and then I shall leave you to prepare for your date.'

Despite her nervousness Natasha caught the edge to his voice and her heart leapt once more.

He was angry.

Serve him right.

Let him stew in his own juice for a while. She would not succumb to him to be abandoned, thrown out like an old rag, or treated like her ancestor. The mere thought of what the previous Natasha had sacrificed for his forefather only to be humiliated for the rest of her life was warning enough, surely?

'I shall be going to England for a few days soon,' she remarked. 'I have a number of loose ends to tie up and friends to see. Everyone is very surprised at my decision to stay in France.'

'I'm sure they must be. I was surprised myself. I think it is very courageous of you,' he added, his expression changing to one of admiration. 'It takes guts to walk into a situation like this and not shy off like a frightened filly. But you're not a frightened filly, are you, Natasha?' He rose, and before she could move was drawing her into his arms. 'You're not frightened, just inexperienced,' he murmured, his hand slipping into the small of her back and pressing her body to his. 'You know that I want you just as I know you want me. Why bother to deny it? You enjoyed the other night as much as I did. Admit it.' He gazed down arrogantly at the top of her head.

'I—' Natasha stared at his chest and clenched her fists. 'I'm not in the habit of simply scratching an itch,' she replied through gritted teeth. 'I think what happened between us was a mistake. One that should not be repeated.'

They were the hardest words she'd ever spoken to him, but despite the scent of him, the temptation to lift her lips and receive his kiss, Natasha stood firm.

Raoul stiffened. 'What do you mean a mistake?' His hold on her tightened. 'You call this a mistake?' In one swift movement his hand slipped under her chin and he tilted her face up. Then, before she could react, his lips came down firmly on hers, parting them, forcing her to open up to him, to allow him in where she'd vowed she wouldn't.

She could feel the hardness of his arousal against her abdomen, felt herself go liquid inside, felt her nipples ache against his chest, was yearning for that feathery caress, an easing of the tightness that was spiralling within her.

'This is no mistake,' Raoul growled, lifting his mouth from hers and staring deep into her eyes while his fingers found her breast, 'and neither is this,' he muttered, slipping his hand deftly below her sweater, a triumphant smile breaking as he felt her braless nipple peak under his grazing thumb. 'I will teach you how to recognize a mistake, *mademoiselle*,' he whispered, taunting further, making sure she felt him as his other hand slipped under the elastic of her sweatpants. The smile turned into an arrogant grin as he realized she wore no panties, and his hand roamed freely.

Natasha flushed, felt his fingers come into contact with the delicious welcoming wetness between her thighs and tried to resist, to protest. But once again his lips were on hers. She felt drunk on emotion, high on sensations spiralling, curling within her, felt his expert touch caressing each needy spot inside her until she was gasping in his arms, begging for fulfilment.

'Not so fast, *chérie*,' he muttered, taking it slowly, prolonging the delight. 'Not so fast. When you come I want you to be damn certain that this is no mistake.'

Then when she could bear it no more his fingers quickened their pace, bringing her over the edge, making her cling to him, dizzy with pleasure, unable to do more than lean her head against his broad chest and allow him to take her in his arms and sit her on his knee on the sofa.

Before she had time to recover he'd slipped off her pants and was quickly undressing himself.

'Raoul,' she begged weakly, 'this is crazy. Someone could come in. I—'

'Shush,' he ordered, lying on top of her and easing himself inside.

'Ahh.' Natasha sighed as he entered her, feeling him fill her and knowing it felt so right. For a moment Raoul lay thus, staring down at her, their bodies as one. Then with slow methodical thrusts he had her gasping again, raising her hips to his as together they discovered a new and wonderful rhythm that she wished would go on and on for ever. She forgot where she was, the time and place, simply gave way to the delight of his lovemaking, drawing him further and further within her until at last they came in a frenzied rush and Raoul sank on top of her.

They lay, spent, hearing the beat of each other's heart. But after a few minutes reality began to sink in and Natasha took stock of her situation. Here she was, half-naked, lying in the arms of one man while expecting another to take her to dinner at any minute.

'Raoul,' she whispered, touching his shoulder.

'Mmm,' he grunted.

'Raoul, we must get dressed. Gaston will arrive at any moment and I'm not even ready.'

She felt him stiffen, then raise himself. His dark hair was tousled and his eyes turbulent as he stared down her.

'You mean you still intend to go out with Mallard after what just occurred here?' he bit out, eyes blazing.

'I have to. I accepted his invitation. It would be very rude to cry off at the last minute.'

There was a moment's silence before he withdrew himself in one quick movement and rose. 'I should have expected this,' he exclaimed jeeringly. 'They say like mother like daughter. In your case,' he said bitterly, pulling on his clothes, 'I should say like ancestor like descendant. It is obviously not just Natasha's name you inherited, but her nature as well.' With that he dragged his fingers through his hair and, sending her one last fulminating glance, marched from the room.

Bewildered, Natasha hastily pulled on her clothes as the sound of his car engine disappeared into the night. This was all too crazy, too ridiculous for words. Here she was being accused of...what? What exactly was he accusing her of?

She ran upstairs to her room and hastened to the shower. Gaston would be here any minute.

How could she possibly face him after what had just happened?

Oh, Lord.

This was all so confusing, so unsettling. Hadn't she promised herself not to submit to Raoul's advances again? Yet at the first opportunity she'd faltered. And now he was accusing her of being like her ancestor. Well, he could be easy on that score, she reflected with a sniff, letting the hot jet of water soothe her satisfied body. She would not let what had happened to her ancestor happen to her. Would not be despised and humiliated, however hard he tried.

With a determined huff Natasha dried herself with a large terry towel and, grabbing a pair of jeans and a silk shirt from her closet, pulled them on just as a flash of headlights illuminated the night.

Gaston was here.

Oh, God.

She would have to use all her British *sang froid* to keep her cool tonight, she realized, taking a deep breath. Too bad if Raoul was upset that she was dining with Gaston. He was being ridiculous. Surely he must realize she would be incapable of doing anything with another man? The realization hit her hard and she swallowed.

Was she really that badly smitten?

CHAPTER FOURTEEN

RAOUL drove back to the Château in a towering rage.

How dared she flout him like this? How dared she go from his arms to the company of another man? He should have known. Hadn't history warned him enough? Weren't the circumstances recounted to him since childhood sufficient warning to keep him away from her?

'Bon sang!' he exclaimed, ramming his foot on the accelerator angrily. That he, a seasoned womanizer, should get caught in a trap like this. Destiny surely had something to do with it. And she'd said she'd seen Natasha's ghost. Perhaps there was more to it than met the eye. Perhaps the old Natasha had come to take revenge on his ancestor through him.

He shook his head and told himself to stop being ridiculous. This was the twenty-first century, after all. He must simply bring an end to this damn nonsense and leave for Paris immediately. Perhaps he should just marry

Camille de Longueville, whose mother had been pushing her at him for the past months, and have a traditional French marriage with several mistresses on the side and be done with it.

Right now, he reckoned, furious, anything would be better than this.

'You seem tired tonight,' Gaston remarked as they finished dessert.

'Oh, just a little,' she evaded, mustering a smile. Where was Raoul? On his way to Paris by now, probably.

'Well, maybe it's the sudden change in temperature,' Gaston replied blandly. 'It has become quite cold for the season.'

'Yes. I suppose it has,' she answered vaguely. What if he'd left in anger and had an accident on the road? It would be all her fault.

'Natasha?' Gaston leaned across the table and touched her hand. 'You seem very far away. Is something troubling you?'

'I'm so sorry,' she said, blushing, realizing how rude she must appear. 'I was just distracted by something.'

'Some*thing* or some*one*?'

Her eyes flew up. 'I—'

'You don't need to explain,' he said, squeezing her hand. 'I caught the vibes between you and Raoul yesterday. It is quite obvious that the two of you are very attracted to one another.'

'Is it?' She looked squarely at him now, her eyes big with wonder. 'I didn't realize that other people were aware.'

'My dear, this is France,' he replied, with laughter in his eyes. 'Romance is in the air. It is the first thing we sense between a man and a woman.'

'Oh, gosh. It's all so difficult.' Her shoulders slumped.

'Why? Or rather, why don't you tell me about it?' Gaston sat back and smiled at her. 'I am your friend, Natasha, I'm here to help. I am also Raoul's friend, and I get the feeling that something isn't right between you two.'

'You're only too right. It isn't.' She sighed, leaned her elbows on the table and steepled her fingers.

'Then let me order a couple of calvados and you shall tell me about it.' He raised a finger and beckoned the waiter.

'There's nothing much to tell, really. We met, and we—I—well, we sort of ended up attracted to one another,' she mumbled, not knowing what else to say.

'And then? You made love?'

Colour flew to her cheeks. 'How did you know?'

'It's written all over you. You made love, and now part of you regrets it because Raoul is a selfish bastard who has no desire to commit to anything. You, on the other hand, are a loyal and trustworthy woman who would not have made love with him were you not emotionally involved. Am I right?' His blue eyes penetrated hers, filled with warmth and understanding.

'That just about sums it up.' She nodded glumly. 'I don't know why I let myself get involved with a man like that. It's crazy. It never should have happened.'

'Why not? It is the unusual in life that attracts us, not the banal. Or not people like you and Raoul anyway.'

'Raoul is obsessed with the past. He seems to have some fixation about that story between

Regis and my namesake. It's almost as if it haunts him.'

'Perhaps it does,' Gaston responded thoughtfully, picking up the glass of calvados and taking a sip. 'You know, the Argentans are a very proud and noble family. They never forgave my ancestor for taking the lovely Natasha's virginity for Regis's life. To them, it constituted the ultimate humiliation. Raoul still thinks of it thus. We used to talk about it some years back, about how funny it was that we could be such good friends when our ancestors had been mortal enemies.'

'Well, just be careful he doesn't become your mortal enemy now. He knows we're dining together tonight,' she said, with a humourless laugh.

'And was not pleased?'

'That's putting it mildly.' She rolled her eyes heavenwards. 'He was furious, and left in a rage saying I was just like the first Natasha,' she ended, deflated.

'I see. Well...' Gaston pondered a moment, then smiled, 'I wouldn't set too much store by Raoul's temper. It flares up, then subsides just as quickly. And I'm a big boy. I can deal with

Raoul's tantrums. Also, it won't do him any harm to realize he's not the only kid on the block.'

Despite her anxiety and nervousness Natasha laughed. 'It's so funny hearing you use American expressions,' she said, smiling, more relaxed now that she had opened up to this man whom she was fast considering to be a good friend.

'I like them. They are most descriptive. But, coming back to the subject at hand, *chère amie*, I would not be surprised if Raoul isn't angry because he has stronger feelings for you than he intended.'

'Do you really think so?' Natasha looked across at him doubtfully. Raoul's behaviour hadn't led her to believe anything except that he wanted his cake and to eat it.

'I cannot be certain, but I think there's a good chance.'

'Well, whatever it is will have to wait,' she said, gazing down into her glass. 'I'm off to England for a few days. I need to settle my affairs there if I'm coming to live permanently in France.'

'Of course you must. Also, getting away will allow you to get a better perspective of the situation.'

'Gaston, there is no situation. Just a hot and heavy physical attraction that got out of hand. I think the sooner I realize that the better it will be for all concerned.'

Gaston shrugged. 'As you wish. Of course only time will tell, *ma chère*.'

That night, as she lay tucked under the covers listening to the wind and rain buffeting the Manoir's solid stone walls, Natasha thought back to every incident she'd experienced since coming to France: her first meeting with Raoul in the field, followed by her grandmother's sudden death—and her new life. It was all very bewildering that, in the space of a few days, her life had taken such a radical change of direction.

She sighed, letting her mind rest for just a moment on the incredible lovemaking of earlier this evening. They could so easily have been caught *in flagrante*. She smiled in the dark, wondering what Henri would have said and done had he walked in on them. Then, turning on her side, she closed her eyes and tried not to wonder where Raoul was precisely at this moment and go to sleep instead.

It was odd walking into her old flat in South Kensington, for now it formed part of another era of her existence. She had contacted the offices of the organization she'd worked for in Africa and regretfully handed in her resignation several days previously, but there were still a number of issues to be dealt with.

As she flipped through the post lying on the floor behind the front door Natasha realized that she felt no nostalgia. Not that she'd ever spent much time here, she admitted, sitting down at the small dining table and depositing the pile of envelopes there while she glanced around the place. It had been more of a *pied à terre* than anything else—a place to drop off stuff, and pick up mail.

An address, but never a home.

She had sold the home near Oxford that had belonged to her parents shortly after the accident, knowing she couldn't bear to live there among the memories. Now she realized that everything that had occurred had conspired to prepare her for the huge change that was about to set her life into a tailspin. Even the lease on this flat was practically up, as though it too was ready to move on and fit in with her new life and plans.

Tonight she would stay home and answer some of the mail, and then she'd begin clearing out the apartment, Natasha decided, pulling her hair back into a ponytail. Then later she would pop down the road to the small Italian restaurant that she'd used to frequent whenever she was in town and say hello to Mamma Gina, the owner. Surprisingly, the restaurant was one of the few things she'd truly miss, she realized, opening the hall cupboard and grimacing at the mess inside: old backpacks, sandals, windbreakers and sunhats—all the stuff she'd needed in her previous life which now seemed so remote. Perhaps she should make up a big parcel and send it all to the Salvation Army.

Bracing herself for an afternoon of sorting, Natasha entered the kitchen and took out two large plastic rubbish bags.

'Better get on with it,' she muttered to herself, rolling up her sleeves. No time like the present.

*   *   *

'What do you mean, she's left?' Raoul snapped down the phone.

'Just as I said, Monsieur le Baron,' Henri answered patiently. '*Mademoiselle* said that she was leaving for a few days.'

'Did she say where she was going?' There was a moment's hesitation. 'Well? Come on, man,' he urged impatiently, 'where is she?'

'I am not at liberty to say.'

'Not at— What on earth do you mean, Henri? This is *me* you are talking to you, not some stranger.'

'I know, Monsieur le Baron,' Henri replied uncomfortably. 'But *mademoiselle* gave special orders not to disclose her whereabouts.'

'I quite understand. Quite right. Can't have strangers knowing all one's moves. So where is she?'

'Monsieur le Baron, I have just told you that I am not permitted to say.'

All at once the penny dropped, and Raoul sat up straighter behind the desk. 'Are you saying,' he asked deliberately, 'that *mademoiselle* left specific orders not to tell *me* where she was going?'

'That's it, sir.' Henri was obviously relieved that Raoul had finally understood. 'She was quite adamant about it.'

'She was, was she? Thank you, Henri.'

He laid the phone back in its cradle, leaned back thoughtfully in the deep leather office chair and twiddled his Mont Blanc pen. So she was running away. Had had the nerve to give orders not to disclose her whereabouts.

'Ha!' He let out a harsh humourless laugh. As if he was interested in her damn whereabouts. The woman had a nerve. Hadn't he immediately left for Paris after her abominable behaviour the other day? Hadn't he made it clear when he'd departed that he wanted nothing more to do with her?

Perhaps, he admitted, letting the chair swing back to its normal position, but it still didn't explain why he couldn't get the wretched creature out of his mind. Her image haunted him. And to make matters worse he'd been out with three different girls, each one prettier than the other, and had deposited all three of them on their doorsteps by eleven in the evening, aware that he had no desire to make love with any of them.

Things were bad when it came to such a pass.

And something must be done.

Urgently.

As far as he was concerned there was only one way of dealing with these *affaires de coeur*. Once you were bitten you had to live it out. He needed to find Natasha, persuade her to go off with him—say to the Caribbean for a couple of weeks—and make love to her endlessly to satisfy the yearning he was experiencing. After that, once he'd had her in every way he'd been imagining for the past few days and nights, he would be over it and would be able to resume his existence without further disturbance.

The only problem with this most laudable plan was that A: he had to get Natasha to cooperate—though he didn't doubt that with a little persuading he could manage that—and B: he hadn't a clue where to locate her.

'Merde alors!' he exclaimed, rising and pacing the large high-ceilinged office like a caged leopard. Imagine disappearing in this unusual manner and then having the nerve to leave specific instructions not to inform him. *Him!* It

was unheard of. No sooner had he turned his back on her than she was up to something. Well, not for long, he vowed, an idea shaping in his fertile brain.

Stopping in front of the desk, he picked up the phone and dialled.

'Hello, Gaston, *comment vas-tu?*'

'Very well. And you? Are you here?'

'No, I'm in Paris. But I'll be back at the Château in a few hours. Doing anything tonight?'

'Nothing special.'

'Then how about a bite of dinner?'

'Sounds good, *mon ami*. Where?'

'At my place,' Raoul responded, taking a sudden decision. He wanted to be on home turf for the conversation he was going to have later that evening.

Of that he had no doubt.

CHAPTER FIFTEEN

'WELL, well— Santa Maria, that is an amazing tale you just told me.' Mamma Gina wiped her hands on her red and white checkered apron, took a sip of the wine she'd brought to the table and shook her head, her black and grey curls bobbing.

'I'll miss you, Mamma Gina. In fact, you and the restaurant are the only things I'll miss. London was never my home. None of my friends are here—or not permanently anyway.'

'But of course you are correct to go back to your family's rightful home,' Mamma Gina exclaimed, shocked that Natasha could have doubted for a moment that she had taken the right decision. 'It is your blood—*la sangue*. It is more important than anything. The rest— bah! That is unimportant. Now all you need is to find a good man and settle down in this nice home your grandmother left you and have lots of *bambini*.'

Natasha laughed and shook her head. 'I don't think that's likely to happen any time soon, Mamma Gina,' she replied, smiling.

'But why not? Are these Frenchemen blind as well as crazy? Look at you, *una bella ragazza*, in the flower of youth, ready for marriage. Why, of course you will find a husband soon.'

'Frankly, I'm not looking for one.'

'You say that because you are still angry about Mr Paul,' Mamma Gina said, eyes narrowed and shaking her head wisely. 'He was no good for you.' She gave a demonstrative wave of her hand, relegating the infamous Paul to the past. 'I never like him. He very, very selfish. Not good for you. But you must keep open your heart, Natasha.'

'That's not easy when all the men I meet merely want to go to bed with me and then drop me like a hot potato,' she said with a touch of bitterness, her mind racing back to Raoul and his insupportable behaviour.

'Ah.' Mamma Gina nodded wisely and wagged her finger. 'So there is someone after all.'

'No, there isn't,' she responded, a little too quickly.

'*Eh, va bene.* As you wish.' Mamma Gina rolled her eyes and sighed gustily. 'I don't ask any more questions. When you're ready to tell me you will tell me.' Then she got up and grinned widely. 'Now, you will eat some of Mamma Gina's pasta, *sì*? You look too thin. I think they don't feed you properly in France.'

She bustled off to the kitchen to see to the preparation of the pasta and Natasha leaned back in the booth and sipped her wine, remembering Gaston's words at dinner. It was true that being out of a situation allowed one to view it more clearly. And it was becoming abundantly clear to her that, however painful, she simply must cut Raoul out of her life before he hurt her too badly. The realization that her feelings for him were far stronger than she had at first imagined came as a shock. How had it happened? How had this whole episode transformed from mere attraction into...?

Love?

Natasha set her glass down so sharply that a few drops of wine spilled on to the checkered tablecloth. Surely she must be imagining this.

The feelings she had for Raoul were tempestuous, and they ranged from anger to deep attraction to wondering whether he'd got over the slight cold he'd had when they'd last met. But surely that didn't mean...?

She must definitely banish him once and for all from her existence, she realized, relieved that she'd left Henri instructions not to divulge her whereabouts. She needed time to think, to decide exactly how she would act. But that was almost impossible since Raoul was so erratic.

The main thing, Natasha reflected anxiously, hastily composing her features as Mamma Gina came out of the kitchen door with a plate piled high with spaghetti Carbonara, was to avoid him at all costs. That way, whatever damage had already been done to her heart would be limited.

She hoped.

'Was there a specific reason for you inviting me here to dine?' Gaston asked, coming directly to the point as he accepted a whisky from Raoul and sat in the deep sofa opposite the fire.

'Why would you imagine that?' Raoul queried, eyes narrowed as he leaned against the huge stone mantel.

'Just a gut feeling. I know you very well, *mon ami*. Remember, we've been through a lot together since we were children. I know how you operate.'

'Operate?'

'Exactly. Let's not beat about the bush, Raoul. You invited me here tonight because you don't know where Natasha is and it's driving you crazy.'

'Rubbish.' Raoul stood straighter to disguise his discomfort at his friend's astute summing-up of his motives for inviting him over.

'Isn't that it? Come, come, *cher ami*, this is you and I talking. No need to keep up the façade between old friends.'

'Old friends,' Raoul mused, staring into his glass. 'Yes, we are, aren't we? Yet our ancestors were mortal enemies. All because of another Natasha, to whom this one is related.' His eyes met his friend's full-on. 'I would hate for our friendship to end up in a similar manner. All because of a woman.'

'Are you implying that I'm trying to court Natasha?' Gaston said, an edge to his voice.

'Why not? You've taken her out to dinner; she's a very attractive woman. You know that I'm not interested.'

'Do I?' he challenged. 'Or do you, the Baron, still expect me, the mayor, to ask for your permission to court a woman he considers his? In other words, it's all right if you don't want her any more? I thought *droit de seigneur* went out of fashion with the Revolution.'

'Don't be absurd, and stop pokering up in that ridiculous manner,' Raoul muttered, realizing he'd insulted his friend. 'I meant nothing of the sort. I know you're not the kind of man to undermine his friends.'

'In that case you should know very well that I would never court Natasha, and this conversation shouldn't be taking place,' Gaston said, slightly appeased. 'But you are the one being ridiculous. You are crazy about her, and guess what?' he murmured smugly, taking a long sip. 'I know where she is.'

'Damn it, why did she disappear like that all of a sudden?' Raoul burst out. 'She won't tell me where she's gone. I can't make head nor tail of it. Women,' he exclaimed, rolling his eyes and shaking his head. 'Always complicating what is perfectly simple.'

'I fail to see how Natasha's leaving for a few days complicates anything. Besides, as she pointed out, it's really none of your business.'

Raoul stiffened. 'She said that?'

'Loud and clear.'

'Well, *ça alors*,' he huffed. 'None of my business, indeed. What does she mean by that?'

'Exactly what she said.'

'But I'm her neighbour. I might have a problem between the estates which could require me getting in touch with her urgently. I might—'

'Raoul, are you listening to what you're saying?'

Raoul stopped suddenly, realizing that what he was saying was indeed absurd. Shaking his head, he raised his hands with a shrug and gave in. 'Okay, I admit I've missed her, wondered where she is.'

'Ah, that's better. And, for the record, having deeper feelings for a woman isn't a crime.'

'Who says I have deeper feelings for Natasha? I don't. Remember, she's a Saugure. They betrayed my family once already.'

'If you call giving up your virginity to save the man you love more than life a betrayal,' Gaston remarked sardonically. 'Personally, I would rather have thought of it as heroism. But there, of course, we differ.'

'Because it was *your* ancestor she slept with,' Raoul retorted, casting Gaston a dark look from under his thick brows.

'Raoul, grow up, for goodness' sake. We live in the twenty-first century, not in the midst of the French Revolution. Times were different then. Surely you can understand what was really behind the way those two men interacted?'

'Well, yes, of course I can. Regis was a fool in part, I suppose.'

'A complete fool, who threw away his and Natasha's happiness out of misplaced pride. Just as my ancestor was a bastard who should never have taken advantage of a desperate woman in such a manner. But let's stay in the present. What are your intentions towards the present Natasha?'

'My intentions?' Raoul looked up, surprised. 'What intentions? I like her a lot, that's all. *Ni plus ni moins.*' He shrugged.

'Strange, I had the impression that perhaps you felt more for her than you wish to admit.'

'Put it this way,' Raoul said carefully, swirling his whisky before taking a long sip. 'I'm interested enough to want to know where she is and with whom.'

'*Where* I may be able to help you with. *With whom* I have no idea. Probably on her own, from what I gathered.'

'I see. Did she prohibit you from enlightening me about her destination?' There was a glint in Raoul's eyes as he spoke.

'Not at all. She is in London, tying up some details from her former life and closing her flat.' Gaston threw his arm over the back of the sofa and observed his friend. He could read the conflict, the antagonistic war of pride and emotion. Ah, Raoul. When would he forget the past and wake up to the present?

'Thank you, *mon ami.* I feel relieved to know she is safe. Do you have her address and number, by any chance?'

'Since I was pretty sure that this was why you asked me here tonight, I went to the trouble of writing it down.' Gaston's eyes were filled with understanding mischief as he took a slip of paper from his breast pocket and handed it over. '*Voiçi, mon ami.* Make good use of it.'

Raoul accepted the paper and glanced at it a moment. 'Be sure that I will. *Merci.*'

CHAPTER SIXTEEN

STARING at the pile of boxes filling the small living room, Natasha leaned against the bookcase and took stock of her handiwork. Practically all her former possessions were packed away. She glanced at her watch. The storage company she'd hired would be here to take them away in half an hour. After that there would be little left to do except give the place a final go-over and hand the keys back to the estate agents.

As she was about to put the last items inside the one remaining open box, the doorbell rang. Gosh, the movers had come early.

She hastened to open the door, and a quick gasp escaped her.

'Paul,' she exclaimed, bewildered. 'What on earth are you doing here?' She took an instinctive step backwards.

'Hi. I was in the area and thought I'd drop in, see what you're up to these days.'

'Well, I'm fine,' she responded warily. 'Actually, I'm in the middle of moving.'

'Leaving this place, are you?' He leaned casually against the doorjamb and smiled cheekily at her. He looked unkempt and scruffy, and not for the first time Natasha asked herself what she'd seen in him.

'Paul, I really don't know what you're doing here or why you bothered to come,' she said pulling herself together. 'You left fast enough last time, if I remember rightly.'

'Still sore about that, are you?' He reached up and tweaked her hair.

Natasha pulled back abruptly. 'Look, I'm afraid you'll have to leave now. I have the movers coming in a few minutes.'

'Hoity-toity. Back to our aristocratic little self, are we? Always thought you were better than everyone else at uni, didn't you?'

'Paul, don't be ridiculous. Just go away and leave me alone. I'm busy, and we really have nothing left to say to each other.'

'Says who?' He stood straighter. Suddenly he was looming over her, leering down at her, and Natasha realized he was drunk. Fear shot through her. She was here alone. What if—?

At that moment Paul reached down and yanked her towards him.

'Stop it!' she cried, pushing her hands against his chest. 'Leave me alone and go away. You have no right to come here.'

'Now, now, don't get snotty with me, Miss Smarty-pants. I'll show you who's in charge here.' He forced her against him and his mouth clamped down on hers.

Natasha fought vainly, the futility of her plight all too clear. For although Paul was thin and lanky he was also strong and wiry, and there was little she could do to prevent his attack.

Raoul stood at the bottom of the stairwell and glanced at the piece of paper. Second floor.

It was only as he was climbing the stairs that he heard a scuffle and a muffled cry from above. Hastening his step, he took the stairs three at a time. When he came across Natasha struggling in a man's arms his reaction was quick and thorough. He grabbed the man by the scruff of his T-shirt collar and yanked him off her so fast that Paul didn't know what had hit him. In another swift and accurate move he sent him rolling down the stairs.

'Didn't you hear the lady?' Raoul enquired icily of the whimpering creature lying prostrate on the landing below. 'Now, get out, and don't ever come back—*salop.*'

Then he turned and eyed Natasha, who stood shaking in the doorway. She looked very young and vulnerable in an old T-shirt and faded jeans, tennis socks and a ponytail. 'Are you okay?' Raoul asked, frowning. He wanted to move forward, take her in his arms and make sure she was all right, but something stopped him. 'Who is that bastard?' he demanded.

'My old boyfriend,' she whispered.

'Ah.' Raoul nodded, came inside and, taking her arm, led her into the living room where he sat her down on the sofa. 'I'll get you a drink. Do you have anything here?'

'No, just water.'

'Right.' He moved quickly towards the kitchen and poured her a glass.

'Drink this,' he commanded.

Too shocked to do otherwise, Natasha did as she was told. The water soothed her. 'I don't know why he turned up here today. I haven't seen him for years, and then suddenly out of the blue, on the day I'm moving, he appears.'

'In France we say that bad grass—*les mauvaises herbes*—has a habit of popping up when least wanted,' he answered dryly, looking down at her, his eyes filled with concern. So this was the bastard who'd hurt her. Now he wished he'd taught him even more of a lesson.

Sitting next to her, Raoul slipped an arm around Natasha's shoulders. 'Now, calm down, *ma petite*. It's all over. He won't be back any time soon.'

'No. Thanks to you, I don't think he will,' she agreed, a shy smile hovering as she turned and looked at him. 'Thanks for what you did. But how did you know I was here?' She frowned, remembering her instructions to Henri.

'Oh, I have my ways and means of finding things out when necessary,' he said, touching her cheek and smiling down at her. 'Now, tell me, what is all this packing?'

'I'm leaving this flat and the movers should be here any minute.'

'And where do you plan to go tonight?' he enquired, interested.

'I don't know. Actually, I hadn't really thought about it. I—'

Raoul pulled out his cellphone and rose to his feet, punching in numbers as he did so. 'Is that the Berkeley? Peter—good afternoon. I'll need you to reserve a suite on the same floor as mine. It's for Mademoiselle de Saugure. Yes, we'll be arriving in a couple of hours. You do have one available? Perfect.' He ended the call. 'Well, that's settled. No need to worry about accommodation.'

'Raoul, I never said I wanted to go to the Berkeley,' she protested, torn between annoyance and amusement at his high-handed manner.

'Why not? It's a perfectly respectable establishment, I assure you.'

'I'm very well aware that it's a perfectly respectable establishment, but that's not the point—'

'Then what is?' he asked, eyes dark as he drew her up into his arms. 'Is there somewhere else you'd prefer to go? If so, tell me and I shall cancel everything, *chérie*. Your wish is my command.'

'I give up,' Natasha exclaimed, rolling her eyes and glancing again at the boxes. 'Raoul, I really have to get this finished.'

'Fine. Then I shall sit here and watch you.'

'Couldn't I just meet you later? I'll grab a cab when they've gone.'

'And risk having that creep return? *Non, non.* No way can I permit that. I shall stay, whether you like it or not. I'm afraid you're stuck with me.'

'Oh, very well.' Natasha let out a sigh and, realizing she must finish off quickly, got down to the task of checking every last drawer, nook and cranny where some item might have been forgotten. She was conscious of Raoul in the room, conscious of how physical he made her feel. How was it that just the feeling of Paul close to her had caused nothing but repugnance and disgust, yet Raoul's closeness sent delicious shivers running through her?

Several minutes later two burly men arrived from the moving company, and soon there was nothing left in the apartment but a few memories, most of which she had no regrets at leaving behind.

'Right. I'm ready to go,' Natasha said, turning to Raoul.

'Are you sure? No regrets at leaving this part of your life behind you?'

'Actually, no. It was time.'

'Good. Then let's get going.'

Placing his hand lightly at her elbow, and picking up her duffle bag in the other, Raoul steered her out, and she locked the door behind her for the last time.

CHAPTER SEVENTEEN

HARRY'S BAR was packed that evening, but of course Raoul had been kept one of the best tables in the corner, from where they had a full view of the restaurant.

Natasha noticed several notables, one famous rock star and two royals, seated not far from them. It amused her how everyone treated Raoul so deferentially. No wonder he was so sure of himself. He took it all for granted, as though it was his right. Perhaps he wasn't so different from Regis after all, she reflected, hiding a half-smile as she studied him from behind the menu while a little voice inside told her to take heed of this last thought. Regis had deprived her ancestor of true happiness, thanks to his insufferable pride. It would be too easy for his descendant to do the same.

Telling herself not to imagine things, Natasha concentrated on the choice of dishes, deciding on potted shrimp followed by Dover sole. A bit fishy, perhaps, but two things she loved and would not be having in France. Not that she planned to abandon England; in fact, the thought of acquiring a small flat here had occurred to her.

But not now. Later, maybe.

Right now she needed to focus on getting the estate into good order and enjoying the flat in Paris and the villa in Eze that her grandmother had bequeathed her.

Once they had ordered Raoul seemed more relaxed, as though he'd dealt with an important issue and could now focus on her. She noted that whatever or whoever he focused on was given his full attention. She was, Natasha realized ruefully, taking an awful lot of notice of Raoul d'Argentan's habits.

'So. You like Harry's Bar?' he asked, slipping his hand proprietorially over hers.

'I think it's delightful. I've never been here before. My father and I always used to go to the Savoy Grill together.'

'Ah, an excellent choice. But without your father it is not as charming as it used to be?'

'No. I decided not to go back. I'd rather keep the memories intact.'

'You are right. It is always better so. *Le passé* is the *passé* and should stay that way.'

'You haven't ever spoken to me of your past,' she remarked, discreetly removing her hand from his.

'You mean my childhood?' He raised his brow and smiled, that same intense smile that left her swallowing and taking a quick sip of the delicious Pouilly-Montrachet that the sommelier had poured them.

'Yes. What was it like growing up in a fortress?'

'No different than growing up anywhere else, I imagine.'

'Surely it must have been. Not many people have that opportunity. It's a very different life, after all.'

'Different from what? How would I know the difference? I never lived anywhere else,' he said with a nonchalant shrug.

'No. I don't suppose you would see the difference,' she said dryly, thinking of all the children she'd looked after in Africa and their deprived backgrounds.

As though reading her thoughts, he responded, 'That does not mean that I am not aware that I have been very privileged to be born with—what is it you call it in English?—a silver spoon in my mouth?'

'Something like that.'

'My mother was very conscious of making me aware of my good fortune. That is why I have many friends in the village. People like Gaston, for instance. We went to the village school together until we were twelve.'

'What happened after that?'

'I went to L'Ecole des Roches. It is a prestigious boarding school. The equivalent of your Eton.'

'And Gaston?'

'He came too.'

'Really?'

'My parents insisted that we both have a similar opportunity in life. My father paid his school fees.'

'That was nice of him.'

'Nice? I don't know about nice. It was the right thing to do. Gaston was a far better student than I ever was. He deserved the opportunity. He is a very bright man. But apparently you know that, as you have seen quite a lot of one another, *n'est-ce-pas*?'

'I wouldn't say a lot, but some,' she demurred, realizing he was fishing and determined not to fall into the trap.

'Don't you find him charming?' Raoul's eyes bored through her as though he were searching her soul.

'I find him a very nice man. I think he's a good friend. Well, you should know that.'

'Yes, he is. But there is no friendship where a woman is concerned.'

'What do you mean?' She stiffened.

'Merely that when a man and a woman are interested in one another, friendship often falls by the wayside.' He drank, peered at her over the rim of his glass, studying her closely.

'Is that what you think?'

'Yes. It is.'

'Perhaps you should be more trusting,' she replied coldly, 'and not underestimate people. And if you're implying that Gaston made a pass at me you'd be making a big mistake. Not that it's any of your business,' she added, taking a deep breath and looking stonily at her plate. Gosh, the man had a way of getting on her wrong side.

'Now, now, *ma chère* Natasha, don't get upset with me. I wasn't implying anything at all.' His hand strayed towards hers once more but she slipped it neatly under the table. 'Are you cross with me?' He tilted his head with a disarming smile.

'I'm not cross, Raoul, just fed up with you always trying to manipulate people and situations.'

'*Moi?* Manipulate?' He looked honestly shocked and she could have laughed out loud at his outraged expression.

'Yes. You like to organize everyone and everything around you like pawns on a chessboard.'

'*Vraiment!* That is ridiculous. I am the most tolerant of persons. Why, I am all for liberty and—'

'Fraternity and equality?' she teased, laughing, unable to stop herself. 'Why, Raoul, don't you think it's time you did a reality check?'

'Now you tease me,' he said, seeing her eyes filled with mirth. Why, this woman was not only lovely and sexy and delicious, she was intelligent too. The thought was somewhat discomforting. He avoided intelligent women on principle. Janine, he recalled, echoes of the past hovering, had been highly intelligent. And much good it had done him.

'Sorry, just having a little fun at your expense.'

'Be my guest, *ma chère*, I have a sense of humour.'

'Yes, you do.' And it's one of the things I so like about you, she thought regretfully as the waiter placed the potted shrimp and buttered brown bread on the table.

'I don't know how you eat those things,' Raoul remarked as he cut a morsel of warm *foie gras*.

'It's typically English and I won't get much of it in France, I suppose.'

'Natasha, should you desire it I will have a shipment delivered immediately to the Manoir.' He reached for her hand and raised her fingers to his lips.

'I don't think I'm that desperate for potted shrimp,' she replied, laughing. The atmosphere, the companionship and the smooth wine were all setting her more at ease than she ever could have imagined.

The dinner progressed in this same vein, with light banter and amusing small talk, the comings and goings of elegant fellow diners, the bustle of efficient waiters and waitresses serving one delicious dish after the other. Soon they had finished dessert and were ready for coffee.

'How about having coffee and an after-dinner drink back in one of our suites?' he said, suddenly smiling.

'Why not?' she replied, liking the idea.

Moments later, as Raoul summoned the waiter for the bill, she began having second thoughts. Perhaps it wasn't a good idea. She was asking for trouble. She should avoid situations that—

All of a sudden Natasha pulled herself up with a jolt.

Damn all her sensible reasoning. Who was she trying to fool? She wanted the man, didn't she? Was more than halfway in love with him. And if the truth be told she knew that she would spend tonight in his arms. It would be the last time she allowed herself to do so. Forget rational thinking for tonight, she ordered herself, and enjoy it.

If only for a while.

CHAPTER EIGHTEEN

As THEY stepped out of the car at the hotel the night air felt cool against her skin, and for a moment Natasha shivered. What she was about to do was unlike anything she'd ever done before. Except with Raoul, she admitted, remembering their time at the cottage. But she'd never *consciously* decided to make love with a man. Particularly knowing that it was not a serious relationship; that there was no commitment.

'Are you cold?' he asked, slipping his arm protectively around her shoulders as they entered the lobby and walked up the few stairs to the elevator.

'I'm fine,' she answered, wishing it was true. All at once her stomach felt odd and her head dizzy. The scent of him so close, the feel of his arm around her and the protective aura of his presence seemed suddenly all too much. She was foolish to have allowed herself to get into this position again. For in the end she was the one who was going to get hurt. And the deeper she got in, the harder the fall and the more intense the pain would be.

As the elevator climbed to their floor Raoul looked down at her, sensing the tension. There was no pretence between them tonight. They both knew what they were about to do. And he liked it that way, liked the fact that he now controlled the situation, and that they understood one another.

Game-playing was over.

It made matters so very much easier. Yet he felt something in her being that was not in entire accord with her decision. And, despite his desire to pay no attention, it bothered him.

'Is something wrong?' he asked finally as they walked down the corridor to his suite.

'No, everything's fine,' she lied.

'I don't think you're telling the truth, Natasha. Something bothers you.' He stopped, looked at her hard. 'If you are not happy, tell me,' he ordered, in that autocratic manner that made her smile.

'I'm fine, really.' She mustered a bright smile. After all it was she who had given the signal, she who had made up her mind. It was silly to spoil what she herself had opted for.

'Good.' He looked her over once more, then smiled back, banishing any doubt and concentrating on slipping the card key in the lock.

'Shall we skip coffee and have a drink?' he suggested, taking off his jacket and slipping it over the back of a chair.

'Great.' Natasha sat down on the sofa, slipping off her pashmina, determined to feel at ease and sophisticated, as though she did this all the time. She thought fleetingly of her friend Melina, who dated different men constantly and had no problem enjoying sex with them. Why couldn't she just think of it like that? As a moment of pleasure.

But as she watched him prepare two brandies, she had to force herself not to experience a rush of something so deep and so intense that it made her feel faint. She swallowed. How had this man managed to captivate her as she was sure he had so many others—women he then dropped as soon as he'd had his fill of them?

Stop it.

Angry with herself, Natasha forced another bright smile and patted the sofa invitingly.

He didn't need to be asked twice.

Raoul sat next to her and, after placing the brandies on the coffee table before them, wasted no time in taking her into his arms.

Ah, she was delicious, he reflected, lowering his lips slowly to hers, nibbling them, allowing his fingers to travel down her swan-like throat, trail lightly over the curve of her small yet full breasts, determined to enjoy the extent of what she was offering. Slipping his other hand into the small of her back, Raoul worked on her zipper and then the hook of her bra. When it gave way he let out a satisfied growl, and, slipping the dress off her shoulders, drew back to view his handiwork.

'*Ravissante,*' he muttered, enjoying the sight of her peaking breasts awaiting his attentions, her lips so sensual, just parted, her eyes full of expectation and that slight hesitation he found so terribly tantalizing. He leaned forward and gently pushed her back among the cushions, where she lay, hair splayed over crimson velvet. 'You are too beautiful, *chérie*,' he murmured, lowering his lips to her right breast, taking the nipple delicately between his teeth, satisfied when he heard her quick intake of breath. Tonight he was going to love her fully, as he'd be willing to bet she'd never been loved before.

Drawing back, he lifted a brandy snifter and, tilting it, allowed a few drops to fall on her breast. Then his tongue followed, flicking there. 'Delicious,' he murmured, reaching his fingers towards her other nipple, which he played with, using index finger, thumb and his tongue to drive her wild. He could feel her begin to writhe underneath him, feel the spiral of tension rising within her, knew she must be aching now between her thighs. And he continued slowly, patiently, determining the rhythm, allowing her no choice but to submit entirely to his whim.

'Ahh.' Natasha let out a small cry of pleasure as his tongue and fingers worked magic. And this was just the beginning. She wasn't even fully undressed. He was just ravishing her breasts as though they alone were the pivotal point of his attention. When she could bear it no more, feeling the rush of damp heat burst between her thighs, an involuntary gasp escaped her and she clung to him, her nails digging into the back of his shoulders as though holding on for dear life, an indescribable pleasure ripping through her like a flash of hot lightning. Then, just as quickly, it eased, leaving ripples in its wake. But when she was about to sink back into the cushions she felt him slip her dress and stockings over her thighs. Soon she was lying naked before him.

'Ah, *ma* Natasha,' he murmured, his dark eyes filled with an expression so intense it affected her as much as his fingers. 'Look at you, how lovely, how beautifully you give yourself.' His fingers trailed over the soft white surface of her naked thighs, temptingly close but not quite touching the spot she was dying for him to reach. It was like a delicious torture, a taunting that she wanted to beg him to end yet delighted in. Then to her utter surprise he was kneeling on the floor, and instead of his fingers he lowered his lips to her.

Hands lacing his hair, Natasha cried out as his tongue found her, flicked her most vulnerable sensitive spot as cleverly he discovered her. Then, just as she thought this was more than she could bear, his fingers penetrated, bringing her to such unutterable completion that she shook, her whole body racked with indescribable bliss, her gratification such that all she could do was collapse, her fingers raking his hair, gasping.

Raoul rose and, sitting back on the sofa, took her into his arms.

'Ah, Natasha, you are so beautiful, so lovely, such a complete woman. You were made to be loved by a man who can satisfy your desires. How is it that you waited so long to fulfil them?'

Unable to answer, she lay in his arms, basking in contentment, happy just to savour the moment and not think of anything except the delightful fulfilment she was experiencing. Never in her wildest dreams had she ever thought making love could be anything like this. Nothing, she realized, turning her face into his chest as a rush of tears came over her, could have prepared her for this.

'Are you all right, *ma chérie*?' he asked, stroking her hair with one hand while unbuttoning his shirt with the other.

She nodded silently, unable to speak, too afraid that if she did the spell would break and she would wake up from this wondrous dream.

Soon Raoul was naked too. She could feel his growing desire hard and tense against her thigh, and a new and intense stirring began. Was it possible that after all she'd just experienced she could feel the spiralling excitement quivering once again?

As though reading her thoughts, Raoul rose and lifted her in his arms. 'Time for the real thing,' he said, smiling down at her as he entered the dimmed bedroom and laid her on the large bed, its covers turned down.

Natasha knew it was her turn, that she should pleasure him as he had her. But Raoul didn't give her the chance. When she attempted to reach for him he removed her hand.

'Another time,' he whispered, placing himself on top of her. Parting her thighs, he braced his hands on each side of her and in one quick deep thrust entered her.

Again Natasha gasped, her hips reaching up to meet his. And once again he smiled down at her. 'Not so fast, *mon amour*. Lie back and enjoy. There is time enough for you to join me.' Then, as though by some miracle of witchcraft, he began making love to her slowly, rhythmically, determinedly, easing himself within her, seeking that crucial spot deep inside as though he knew every secret place within her. And Natasha obeyed him, lay back and allowed him to take her on a new incredible journey of discovery.

But suddenly she could bear it no more and, reaching up, she pulled him down on top of her, thighs curling about his hips, crying out for him as they joined in a frenzied, perfect coupling that intensified until all at once, together, they tumbled over the edge of a ragged cliff, gasping, crying with joy as they fell, limp and satisfied, in each other's arms among the rumpled sheets.

Several minutes passed before Raoul opened his eyes and realized he had Natasha pinned beneath him. He was finding it hard to digest the experience. Never in all these years and with all the women he'd been with—and God knew there had been a few—had he experienced anything quite like this. It was fantastic, but also troubling, and he sat up, withdrawing his arm and pulling the sheet over them.

'Are you cold?' he asked, for something to say to restore normality to a situation that, had he not been a down-to-earth, sensible man, he might have believed was magical.

'No,' she murmured, turning on her side, opening her eyes and looking at him in a way that left his already fast-beating pulse leaping.

This was ridiculous.

Absurd.

Usually once he'd made love with a woman he made an excuse to get into the shower and then leave. Yet here he was, unable to stop himself from leaning down and kissing her, stroking her hair, sinking back into the pillows and surrounding her with his arms, curling up against her and holding her close. 'Go to sleep, *ma mie*,' he murmured, giving way to temptation and breathing in the soft, enticing scent of her hair. 'Make sweet dreams.'

Natasha smiled sleepily into the pillow and slipped her hand over the one that was covering her breast. It felt so right, so warm, so wonderful.

And she wished it could last for ever.

CHAPTER NINETEEN

IT WAS autumn now and a panoply of multi-coloured leaves carpeted the wide stone terrace that led from the front façade of the Manoir to the lawn.

Natasha stared out of the study window, unable to pin her thoughts down, unable to concentrate on the bills and accounts she'd had lying on the desk for several days now but which she seemed incapable of addressing.

There had been not a word from Raoul after their return from London. Then all at once he'd phoned and said he wanted to dine with her. Knowing she'd be signing her own death warrant if she accepted, Natasha had forced herself to refuse. She'd been off-hand, almost bored on the phone, leading him to believe that she was very busy and had little interest in his company.

But nothing could have been further from the truth. Not an hour passed without something sparking her memory, reminding her of the passion they'd shared, making her want to rush to the phone and say that she'd changed her mind. When he'd phoned her again, two days later, and asked if she'd like to join him in Paris for the Prix de l'Arc de Triomphe race at Longchamps, she'd wavered. Surely it wouldn't be so bad just to see him? After all, it was a day event, with other people. Surely she could handle that?

Now, with dusk gathering, she rose and went into the hall. Henri and his wife were out for the day and the house was empty. Natasha switched on the hall lights. She really must do something about the lighting in this place. The electricity was dicey at best. As though divining her thoughts, two bulbs on the immense chandelier looming over her suddenly popped. She sighed and headed for the stairs, lit by the glow of the picture lamps. As she placed her foot on the first step Natasha stared towards the top of the stairs and drew in her breath.

Surely she must be dreaming.

There, descending the stairs and coming towards her, was the same delicate outlined image she'd seen once before. But this time it was clear. She could distinguish the pale blue hue of the satin dress, the sparkle of something at the woman's throat. It was as if her ancestor was trying to speak to her, to convey some important message. But what?

Natasha stood in a trance for what felt like minutes, and when her thoughts cleared she stared intently up at her namesake's image, straining to hear her thoughts across the centuries. She looked closer at the portrait and it was as if the woman smiled down at her, encouraging her to listen to a message Natasha couldn't hear.

It made no sense, Raoul reasoned. Hadn't they made love incredibly that night in London? Hadn't they slept together for the rest of the night? Breakfasted together next morning? Then what was the matter with the woman? It was a pity he had been so damn busy, having to make a quick trip to New York and then spend some time in Paris, or he would have already gone over to the Manoir to demand an explanation from Natasha as to why she was behaving so oddly.

Surely they now had an affair going on? One, he admitted, that had both its conve-

niences and inconveniences. On the one hand
it was good to know that she was cloistered at
the Manoir, unlikely to be going out with anyone else. On the other, she was still his neighbour and the whole thing must be dealt with
in a manner which would allow them to extract
themselves from the relationship when the
time came without too much long-term collat-
eral damage.

Now, as he drove thoughtfully up the mo-
torway, Raoul reflected hard on these matters.
She still hadn't said if she was coming with
him to the Prix de l'Arc de Triomphe or not.
Which gave him a perfect excuse to pop over
in a friendly manner to enquire. Yes, he decided as he headed down a country road, that
was what he would do. He wouldn't phone,
but would go over personally instead tomorrow and test the terrain.

Satisfied that he'd come up with the optimal
solution, Raoul drove into the courtyard of his
Château, realizing that he was hungry and
looking forward to dinner. For an instant as he
slipped out of the car he felt a sense of lone-
liness. There was never anyone special to receive him when he got home at night. Not that

this fact had ever bothered him in the past. He shook his head, frowned, and waved to Jean, hurrying towards him.

'*Bonsoir*, Jean.'

'*Bonsoir*, Monsieur le Baron. Did you have a good drive from Paris?'

'*Oui, merci,* Jean. Everything is fine. Any news around here?'

'Well, nothing much.' Jean rubbed his forehead thoughtfully. 'Oh, there was the inauguration of the new organ in the church, of course.'

'New organ? In the church? But how is that possible?' He stopped in his tracks.

'Mademoiselle de Saugure gave the church a new organ in memory of her grandmother, sir. There was a ceremony and a fête in the village. Everybody went.'

Raoul stood still, completely taken aback, then experienced a moment's anger. He had received no invitation to any inauguration, either from the Curé or Natasha. Plus, the Argentans always dealt with church matters.

'Right,' he said, heading towards the door and entering his domain. What the hell was she playing at?

He entered his office, switched on the desk lamp and flipped through his mail absently. The third envelope was an invitation. He opened it. There it was. An invitation to the inauguration. Sent as though he was some *inconnu*, some unknown. She should have personally telephoned him, told him of her plan, found out if it was suitable for her to take such action and gone to the trouble of seeking him out, making sure he was part of the activity. Instead she was treating him in this high-handed manner, as though she owned the damn church.

Well, he wasn't having it.

Turning abruptly on his heel Raoul grabbed an old jacket lying on the chair and marched purposefully back towards the car. Minutes later he was entering the gates of the Manoir and heading up the drive.

When the doorbell clanged Natasha was upstairs, still pondering her strange sensations in front of her ancestor's portrait. Suddenly she became conscious of the ringing bell. Who on earth could it be at this time? She glanced at her watch. It was actually only seven-thirty, but because it got dark much quicker now she was less conscious of the hour.

Making her way down the main stairway, Natasha cast a quick glance up at the portrait. But that was all it was now. A static picture of a late-eighteenth-century woman.

In the hall she reached for the big lock and pulled it back, realizing too late that perhaps she should have found out first who was out there. After all, she was alone in the house. But it was too late for that now.

'Raoul,' she exclaimed in surprise, her pulse leaping.

'Yes. As you see.'

His thunderous expression made her wonder what had upset him. 'Well, I suppose you'd better come in,' she said.

'If it wouldn't be too much trouble,' he replied sardonically.

'I didn't know you were back,' she murmured, letting him past.

'I got back a few minutes ago.'

'I see. Then you must be in need of a drink.'

Raoul ground his teeth and watched her. She seemed calm, cool and collected, and very sure of herself. Not like the woman he'd held quivering in his arms a few weeks ago.

'Yes, a drink would be most acceptable,' he muttered, removing his jacket and flinging it on one of the hall chairs.

'Good, then we'll go to the *petit salon*. I find it's the warmest place in the house. The weather has become quite chilly lately, don't you find?' she commented politely, leading the way into the sitting room.

'Natasha, I did not come here to talk about the damn weather,' Raoul exploded from the doorway.

'No? Then what exactly did you come to talk about, Raoul?' Natasha'a brow flew up in a manner that he was unused to.

'I came here to talk about this—this inauguration in the church that you had the nerve to go ahead with without my authority.'

'Excuse me?' Natasha stood her ground and crossed her arms. 'Did you say *authority*?'

'Yes. You had the impertinence to arrange the inauguration of a new organ to the church, something that has been an Argentan tradition for centuries, without so much as a by-your-leave.'

'Well, if it's an Argentan tradition to help with the church organ, you haven't been attending to it,' she said simply. 'The organ was in an appalling state of disrepair. The poor organist could barely squeeze out a decent hymn.'

'Then it was up to the Curé to tell me.'

'Apparently he's tried several times. But you were always too busy or away. And, as you rarely attend any services in the church, you haven't had the opportunity to hear for yourself,' she responded sweetly. 'Whisky?'

'Yes,' he snapped. 'But that has nothing to do with—'

'Ice?' she interrupted in the same tone.

'No, damn it, water.'

'Good. Because I would have had to fetch the ice from the kitchen, since Henri has the day off,' she said conversationally.

'Natasha, will you stop these witless remarks and listen to what I have to say?' Raoul demanded, his high cheekbones flushed with anger.

'Sorry, I thought I was. Now, you were telling me—or rather were about to tell me—why you had not been upholding your family's tradition properly, weren't you?'

He took two quick steps across the room and before she could stop him pulled her roughly into his arms. 'Stop it,' he ordered.

'Why?' She glared up at him, eyes blazing. 'Because Monsieur le Baron says so?'

'Yes, damn it. You have no right to come here and flaunt our customs. To—to—agh! I don't know how you say it in English.' He turned, threw his hands up and muttered something under his breath in French.

'Why don't you have your whisky and calm down?' Natasha said softly. 'There's no need for all this to-do, Raoul. If I've done something to offend you, I'm sorry. It wasn't my intention. But the organ was in desperate need of renewal and past repair. It seemed to make sense to give the church a new one that would be in place in time for the choir to practise its Christmas repertoire,' she said simply.

The logic of her words sank in. And all at once Raoul realized that he was acting in an inappropriate manner.

He turned, straightening his shoulders. 'It is the duty of the Baroness d'Argentan to attend to such matters,' he said haughtily, accepting the whisky from her. 'My mother was very attentive to such things.'

'I'm sure she was. Unfortunately she is not among us any more, or I'm sure there would have been no need for me to take this measure.'

'Well, I suppose *à la longue* it is for the best,' he muttered grudgingly. 'But I still want to pay for half the organ.'

'I'm sorry, but I've already dealt with it.'

'You cannot deny me that right. It would be a dishonour to the Argentan family if I was not known to have participated in the cost of the instrument. I—'

'Raoul, will you stop thinking that you live in the Middle Ages? Frankly, nobody could care less who paid for the organ. The parish is merely pleased to have the problem solved. The choirmaster is thrilled and Mademoiselle Boisier, who plays the organ, is delighted. I really don't see what you're making such a fuss about. And as for the cost—I can well afford it, thanks to my grandmother's generosity.'

'That is not the point. You don't understand,' he said, taking a long gulp of whisky and shaking his head. 'I told you earlier that you were usurping the place of the Baroness d'Argentan.'

'Really?' She crossed her arms and looked at him, her eyes steady.

'Yes. My mother, and my grandmother before her, were always in charge of attending to these church matters. It was their role. Now you come, a Saugure, and want to take over.'

'I have no such ambition,' she replied coldly, 'and as you are not attending properly to your duties then it is for me to do so.'

'No. It's not,' he snapped back. 'That is the duty of my wife.'

'I wasn't aware that you were married,' she retorted, turning to pour herself a glass of wine, her hand quivering.

Suddenly Raoul stopped dead in his tracks and realized what he'd just said.

My wife.

He'd never thought of having a wife. The idea of Camille de Longueville was nothing but a joke. He raised his eyes, watched

Natasha carefully pouring the wine, and blinked.

Impossible.

He must be dreaming.

Of course he was.

Pulling himself together, Raoul stepped over to where she stood. 'Let me do that,' he said in a friendlier tone.

'Don't worry, it's done, thank you.' Natasha turned around and, avoiding him, went to sit down in the armchair, where there was no chance he could join her.

'I'm sorry if I lost my temper,' he said stiffly.

'Oh, that's fine.' She smiled briefly. 'I can see that it must be difficult to come to terms with several centuries worth of high-handedness, even though we do live in the twenty-first century.'

'I am not high-handed,' he replied deliberately. 'I merely carry out what is expected of me.'

'Quite so,' Natasha replied, hiding her smile behind her glass.

'And there is no need to snicker,' he reprimanded, seating himself opposite.

'I wasn't snickering. I merely find your attitudes amusing.'

'I am glad that I provide you with amusement, *mademoiselle*,' he said sardonically.

'Oh, Raoul, stop taking yourself so seriously,' she exclaimed, laughing despite an attempt to stay solemn. 'If you could see yourself, all pokered up and stiff! Why, I'll bet you look just like your ancestor Regis.'

Raoul looked across at her curiously. 'What prompted you to say that?' he asked, eyeing her closely.

'Nothing.' She shrugged her shoulders. She did not intend to share her recent strange, almost ghostly experience with him. 'Just the way you looked, I suppose, so proud and autocratic. It reminded me of what your ancestors must have been like.'

'I suppose they must have. After all, we have the same blood.'

'Precisely,' she murmured with a sigh. 'So, how long are you here for?'

'I don't know. I haven't made up my mind yet.'

Then, to her surprise, he rose, snapped the glass down on the small Louis Quinze table to his right and faced her. 'I have to go. I'll be in touch.'

With that he marched from the room before Natasha could react, and was out of the door with his jacket before she could do more than step into the hall.

'Well!' she exclaimed, standing with her glass as the front door reverberated behind him. 'If that doesn't beat all.'

CHAPTER TWENTY

RAOUL drove back to the Château at a furious pace. He was too stunned by the thought which had crossed his mind only minutes earlier. In fact, he'd nearly choked on his whisky it was so outrageous.

Marriage.

To think that he could even imagine such a thing as Natasha becoming his wife—when the whole world knew that Argentans and Saugures would never be joined by marriage after what had occurred two centuries earlier. It was so unimaginable as to leave him in shock. Something he had never before experienced.

On arrival at the Château he waved away Jean's offer of dinner, having lost his appetite, and headed back into his office. There he threw himself down on an ancient leather couch before the freshly built fire and stared doggedly into the flames. Then, almost surreptitiously, his eyes rose above the great stone mantel and he stared at the handsome portrait of Regis d'Argentan, standing stiff and proud in a wig and pearl satin, which had been there for as long as he could remember.

'This is all your fault,' he muttered, standing up and facing the painting.

'Yes, it is.'

Raoul stared ahead, but the portrait was exactly the same. Yet he could have sworn that a voice had answered him.

Spinning around, Raoul saw the deep burgundy velvet curtains flutter. The curtains never fluttered; they were too heavy.

'Who is there?' he said, wishing he was armed and realizing that he didn't have a revolver in the desk drawer, even if he could make it over there in time.

Raoul stood rooted to the spot, stunned. Surely he must be dreaming and this must be a figment of his imagination. Ever since he was a child he'd heard stories of the occasional apparition of his ancestors in the Château, but had never given them credence, always believed they were part of the folklore of the place. All good castles needed a ghost, after all.

Sitting down abruptly in an old tapestry chair by the fire, Raoul stared up at the portrait. Then he got up slowly from the chair and went and stood by the window. As his eyes adjusted to the dark he could distinguish the turret where the pennant flew. His family's colours and coat of arms. Was the spirit of Regis trying to tell him something? That it was time to bury the hatchet with the Saugures and finally unite the two families?

He turned back into the room and shook his head, thinking about Natasha, about the nights spent in her arms, about the extraordinary closeness and fulfilment he'd experienced with her, such as he had never known before.

At the thought of her his senses became aroused. Never had he shared such moments with any other woman. Perhaps Regis was right and he mustn't let her go. But still. He was his own master and would make his own decisions.

He was damned if he would be dictated to by a ghost.

CHAPTER TWENTY-ONE

THE racecourse at Longchamps was packed with everything from exotic hats in the private boxes to people in jeans and T-shirts come to bet on one of the biggest races of the year.

Natasha hadn't seen Raoul since the evening when he'd come over and departed so abruptly, and in the meantime she had taken the time to think.

However much it hurt, she must not accept less than everything. For that, she realized, was what she truly wanted from this man. Halfway measures just weren't enough. She wanted to be his wife and bear his children, never mind how odious he could be.

And that, she knew—had understood again from Gaston one evening over a drink—was impossible. The dice had been thrown all those years ago, and the same pride still haunted their lives today. So why had she accepted his invitation to come to the races? Because, as she'd told herself before, there was no danger here of them being on their own?

Probably that was the reason. After all, they were here in his box, with Gaston and his pretty new girlfriend, Victoire, and Raoul's charming cousin Madeleine and her husband Gerard.

'Do look at that amazing hat,' Madeleine said, nudging Natasha. The two women had immediately hit it off and were exchanging an amusing conversation together.

Natasha glanced at Raoul, who had raised his racing glasses the better to see the horses that were coming out for the next race, and thought how sad it was that the past prevented them sharing a future. Not that he'd ever indicated he wanted one, she was hasty to remind herself with a little sigh. He looked so divinely handsome in a dark grey double-breasted suit, his hair swept back in that nonchalant manner she had learned to love, his skin still bronzed from the summer sun, and those hands... Her eyes stopped there for a moment, her heart lurched, and again that warm tingling sensation gripped her. God, when she thought about the magic those hands were capable of arousing she shivered.

Quickly glancing the other way, she caught Madeleine peering carefully at her.

'Be careful of that one,' she murmured, smiling in the direction of her cousin. 'He's a wonderful man, and I love him dearly, but don't get caught in his web. It's too tricky.'

Natasha mumbled something incomprehensible and felt the colour rising to her cheeks just as Raoul turned and offered her his glasses. 'Look over there—the jockey in the green and pink shirt. That's number six, *Grand Amour*, the horse you bet on.'

'Is it really Grand Amour?' Madeleine whispered to him softly, for only him to hear.

Raoul turned and looked at her. 'Shut up, Madeleine, and stop talking rubbish.'

'Now, now, don't get snotty on me—I'm your cousin; I have a right to tease you whenever I feel like it.'

To his relief, Natasha, who was adjusting the glasses, did not overhear the interchange. But Madeleine's words left him troubled.

For several days now—in fact two weeks, to be exact—Raoul had been in a quandary.

Never before had he experienced anything similar. Any other woman would have fallen at his feet at the drop of a hat, only too glad to be invited here, yet Natasha had left him dangling. At first he'd been annoyed, and had thought of ringing her and demanding an immediate response. Then he'd changed his mind and decided to bide his time. This was the first time he'd ever needed time to consider a situation with a woman.

His vision of Regis, and the message he'd sensed from his ancestor, had left its mark. But he was still damned if he would let a ghost dictate his future. He needed to follow his own instincts. Now, as he watched her standing next to him in the box, he suddenly wondered what it would be like to be without her. It was months since he'd broken up with Clothilde, and he hadn't had another steady relationship since. For some strange reason he hadn't wanted one.

Forcing his eyes back to the course, Raoul concentrated on the race that was about to begin. *Grand Amour* was well placed. Seconds later they were following the galloping horses, glad to be distracted.

*   *   *

It was a difficult concept to accept, Raoul admitted to himself later, after spending the better part of the night pacing his library. Difficult to come to terms with. But, like it or not, he must: he couldn't live without her.

It bothered him profoundly to know that he could have become so attached to another human being, so dependent. On the other hand, the knowledge that he could conceive of a lifelong commitment with any woman was so surprising it left him flabbergasted.

What he still didn't know—hadn't allowed himself to ponder too closely—was how Natasha felt about him. Oh, he knew she was attracted to him; that much was obvious. But what about the rest? It was, of course, an honour for any woman to be considered as a prospective candidate for the role of Baroness d'Argentan, he reminded himself. But was Natasha fully aware of precisely what an honour he was planning on bestowing upon her?

After several more minutes' debate Raoul decided there was only one way to find out. He would drive over to the Manoir and explain, carefully and methodically, so that she was fully aware of the facts, what was expected of her. Satisfied that he had come up with a well-thought-out, rational solution, Raoul went on his way.

She had no expectation of seeing him any time soon, Natasha reflected as she stepped out onto the terrace after breakfast for a breath of air. Autumn was here to stay now, the leaves red and golden, the air crisp and cool. She pulled her cardigan about her and moved towards the lawn, where she wandered for a few minutes. There was a lot to do this morning—correspondence to catch up with, and so many other little tasks that needed attending to. Her daily life had filled quickly, with so many different activities it was hard to keep up. Yet even though she was constantly doing, she still found it hard to banish Raoul from her mind, to accept that it was not to be and that it was for the best in the long run.

She let out a long sigh and stuffed her hands in her pockets. Then she looked up and to her utter surprise saw Raoul's tall, determined figure moving towards her across the lawn.

Her breath caught and she smothered the desire to run and throw herself into his strong arms. That was all in the past now.

Raoul was approaching, and she pulled herself together and plastered on a little smile. 'Good morning, Raoul. What brings you here so early in the day?' Her tone was casual and pleasant, nothing more.

'I have something I wish to speak to you about,' he said, taking her hand and lifting it perfunctorily to his lips.

'Oh? Should we step into the office?'

'No. That won't be necessary.' Raoul cleared his throat and looked her over thoughtfully. 'I need you to pay close attention to what I am about to say, Natasha,' he continued in an authoritative tone.

'Very well,' she responded, mystified at the seriousness of his demeanour. 'Is something wrong, Raoul?'

'Uh, no. Not exactly. *Enfin*, in a way there is.'

'And how can I help you?' she said patiently, wondering when he would come to the point.

Standing to his full height, Raoul looked down at her. 'Natasha, I have come to ask you to do me the honour of becoming my wife.'

'Excuse me?' She blinked up at him in amazement.

'I understand your surprise. In truth I am surprised myself.' He smiled self-deprecatingly. 'I had no notion that such a thing would come to pass. Particularly with a woman like you.'

'A woman like me?' Now that the surprise was waning, and she understood the full import of his message, Natasha experienced a mixture of amusement at his arrogance, anger at his nerve, and cool detachment.

'Yes. I had no intention of entering the marital state, but I find I cannot be without you. I am profoundly disturbed by your absence. As you can imagine, this is most unsettling. Not only does it affect my business acumen, but it also disturbs my sleep pattern, not to mention several other things.'

'Really?' she murmured dryly. 'I'm very sorry to hear that.'

'Yes, well, I hope that soon all that will be in the past,' he said with his winning smile. 'I think we shall deal very well, you and I, despite your being a Saugure.'

Natasha avoided his outstretched hand and took a step back. She straightened her shoulders and eyed him askance. 'Frankly, I find it quite amazing that someone with your strong ties to the past and your family reputation would even consider asking me to marry him,' she said, controlling her temper.

'Well, yes,' he replied ruefully. 'As I just said to you, it wasn't an easy decision to take. I had to overcome quite a few qualms.'

'I see. And how did you overcome them, may I know?' she asked sweetly.

'That is another long story, which I will share with you in due course. Suffice it to say that I have decided this to be the best course of action.'

'For whom?'

'Why, for me, of course. And I—'

Natasha's colour heightened and her chin went up. 'Is this supposed to be a compliment?'

'Well, I think that any woman would be honoured. After all, I have one of the oldest names and titles in France,' he replied modestly.

'And you wish me to give you an answer?' She tilted her head, amused now at the sheer arrogance of the man, the utter disregard for anything but his own comfort.

'Well?' He smiled down at her confidently.

'Well, here is my answer,' she said, shoving her hands further into her pockets and looking him up and down scathingly. 'I thank you for thinking of me as a possible—though I gather somewhat unsuitable—candidate for the job of becoming your wife. Unfortunately, I do not find the post alluring. So my answer is a re-sounding no!'

'Excuse me?'

'Exactly what you heard, Raoul. I have ab-solutely no desire to marry a man who is not only full of his own self-importance but con-siders that he is doing me a favour by asking me to marry him. For your information, I'm very happy the way I am. I don't need you, and I can think of nothing worse than becom-ing your chattel. And, let's face it, that's ba-sically what you consider your wife should be-come. Someone ready to hop, skip and jump every time you snap your aristocratic fingers, to be there when it suits you, and to efface herself when it does not.'

'But—'

'I haven't finished.' She raised her hand like a traffic cop, allowing him no chance to speak. 'I imagine that you would also expect me to accept with a blind eye all your affairs and to be thankful for the rest of my days. Not to mention having to be eternally grateful that the Baron d'Argentan would even *consider* me as worthy enough of being offered marriage.'

'Natasha, you are taking this in completely the wrong light. I had no intention of—'

'Insulting me?' she retorted. 'Well, guess what? Not only am I insulted, but I must ask you not to set foot on my property ever again. Is that understood? I think after a few hundred years we Saugures have had just about enough of you. Good day.'

With that she turned around and marched back to the house, slamming the French door behind her.

'*Ce n'est pas possible,*' Raoul muttered, aghast, staring at her retreating figure, trying to assimilate all that had just taken place. Natasha must be mad.

Angrily he marched around the Manoir, got back into his Ferrari and drove off towards the village. Driving slowly down the main street, he saw Gaston seated outside the café and immediately pulled over.

'I need to talk to you,' he said, his mind still bursting with surprised outrage.

'Fine. I'll order you a coffee.'

'Make it a double,' Raoul muttered between gritted teeth as he parked the Ferrari and jumped out.

'So?' Gaston looked him over and raised a brow. 'What's left you in this foul mood?'

'*Who* do you think?' Raoul threw out, dropping onto the basketwork chair and flinging an arm on the small bistro table.

'I haven't the slightest notion.'

'Well, let me put you in the picture.'

'Go ahead,' Gaston said, agog with curiosity.

'I have just—against my better judgement, mark you—asked Natasha to marry me.'

'*Mon Dieu.* Are congratulations in order?'

'No, they are not. She refused me.'

'Ah.' Gaston nodded sagely.

'What? You are not surprised? I just told you that she refused my offer of marriage. It is *incroyable*.'

'Yes. Well, I had a feeling that might happen one of these days,' Gaston replied in a conversational tone.

'Excuse me? I seem to be missing something here.' Raoul sat up straighter and stared his friend in the eye. 'Why the hell did you think anything of the sort? Is my offer not good enough? Why, I have offered her one of the oldest names in France and she refuses!'

'That's where the problem lies,' Gaston answered patiently. 'You see, Raoul, Natasha doesn't give a damn about your noble name.'

'That is ridiculous,' he spluttered, accepting his coffee from the waiter.

'No, it's not. In fact, you should be very flattered.'

'I can't imagine why.'

'Because it is *you* Natasha cares for. Raoul the man. Not the Baron, not the spoiled odious brat, but the sometimes great guy who lies beneath that aristocratic veneer.'

'This is a ridiculous conversation,' Raoul demurred, a cold feeling gripping his gut. Had he got it wrong? Had he missed the boat completely?

'It is not ridiculous, and you know it. For once, my friend, listen to the counsel of one who knows better than you. You are a proud, selfish, egotistical son-of-a-bitch.'

'*Merci.*'

'But you are also my very good friend,' Gaston continued, ignoring the sardonic interruption. 'One I would very much like to see happy. Has it never occurred to you that you should be *begging* that woman to become your wife? That she is the best thing that has happened to you in the last twenty years? Or are you too stupid, too full of aristocratic nonsense, to see what any other man would already have understood a long time ago?' Gaston's eyes blazed into his.

Raoul hesitated, then, placing his coffee cup back in the saucer, leaned forward. 'You really think this, don't you?'

'Yes, I do,' Gaston replied with feeling. 'For goodness' sake, listen to yourself, man. Don't you understand marriage is not about *you, you, you*? It is about both of you. It is about making this woman happy, wanting to love her for ever, to give her everything you can. Love, Raoul. I don't think you know the meaning of the word. Frankly, I'm glad she refused you. You don't deserve to tread the ground she steps on.'

With that Gaston got up abruptly and, throwing a few coins on the table, sent his friend a withering glance. 'Wake up, *mon ami*, before it is too late. You've wasted enough time already.'

Without more ado Gaston marched off down the street, leaving Raoul even more bewildered than he'd been when he sat down.

CHAPTER TWENTY-TWO

How could he be so impossibly odious? Natasha wondered, balling her fists and swallowing the tears that she refused to shed. The man didn't deserve even one solitary tear.

Then why did she feel she was dying inside? Why did the mere sight and thought of him still make her want to melt as though she were an ice cream cone left in the sun?

'Damn him,' she muttered, running upstairs to the privacy of her bedroom where, despite her vow not to cry, she fell onto the bed and indulged in a fit of sobbing.

Ten minutes later she pulled herself together and, sniffing into a tissue, sat up. She wouldn't stay here—couldn't stay here. Not while he was about. Not while there was a very strong risk of banging into him.

She'd refused the man she loved for one very good reason: he obviously didn't love her. He wanted her because it pleased him, because he enjoyed her in bed, because—oh, forget all the reasons. They weren't worth going over.

Natasha rose and, pulling a suitcase from her closet, began randomly throwing clothes into it. She didn't care where she went, but get out of here she must.

Half an hour later she was packed and ready, and giving instructions to the staff. This time she would only give her cellphone number so they could reach her. But not her address. Not that she had one to give, she reflected gloomily, revving the car engine. And she was determined that once she did Raoul was not going to get hold of it.

Of course he should have known that she would run after an incident like this. What a fool he'd been—what an imbecilic fool not to realize what was under his nose the whole time.

He loved her.

Of course he loved her. And he'd thought he'd made that plain to her by asking her to marry him.

But Gaston's words, coupled with his own painful reflections, made him suddenly realize that in truth he had not been very complimentary.

'*Quel idiot,*' he muttered to himself, recalling Natasha's expression as she refused him. And now he'd spoiled everything. For it was obvious that Henri really didn't know where she'd gone this time around, and neither did Gaston or anyone else.

Raoul knew a sudden rush of panic and despair such as he had never before experienced. What if she'd driven off in a nervous state and had an accident? What if, because of him, at this very moment she was lying by the roadside covered in blood, or at the bottom of a ditch?

As the myriad of horrifying images played out, Raoul realized just how much he loved this woman. But what was worse was the dreadful haunting feeling that it was too late. She'd expected something of him and he hadn't come through. In fact he'd made a complete botch of the whole thing.

For the first time in twenty-five years Raoul dropped his head in his hands and recognized that he wished, more than anything, that he could turn back the clock twenty-four hours.

But that was not possible.

Now only a miracle could save the day.

And, even if ghosts could appear to pass on unspoken messages, a miracle was too much to expect.

She drove.

For three hours she simply followed country roads with no particular destination in mind, her being in turmoil, her heart in shreds.

But she knew that, despite the pain, her decision was the right one.

Forget marriage on his terms. She was certain that Natasha would have thought the same. The way he envisaged it, things would have been as bad as they were for her ancestor.

Or worse.

For at least Natasha Senior had had the freedom of choice, whereas she, as his wife, would merely find herself subjected to his dominance. And no way, however much she loved him, could she allow that to happen. It was a sure recipe for unhappiness.

But after several hours of wandering Natasha also came to another conclusion as, stopping by the sea, she got out of the car and took a long deep breath: she couldn't run away. She must go back home to the Manoir and face whatever she had to face. It was her home now, her reality. And whether Raoul was close or not was irrelevant. She must stand firm, head high, on her own terrain and confront the situation. Not flee like a scared rabbit.

After several minutes' walking in the bracing sea air Natasha felt better. Gazing out over the grey waters, she let her mind travel back sixty years, to when these very beaches had been bathed in the blood, sweat and tears of those courageous men who'd so bravely fought for the freedom of Europe. Men who had not faltered, she reminded herself, but who had faced the enemy head-on, just as she must.

Without more ado Natasha got back in her vehicle and, gunning the engine, prepared to drive home, in the knowledge that she too would stand strong.

Whatever the odds.

It was impossible to trace her. No one knew where she'd disappeared to. Should he hire a detective to find her? What if—? Raoul ordered himself to stop imagining the worst and blot out the horrific images that crossed his tormented mind. Perhaps she had merely gone to Paris for the day, or— But then why hadn't she left directions with her staff?

'I don't know where she can be,' he repeated to Gaston for the hundredth time as he paced the Baronial Hall of the Château while his friend sat in one of the high-backed velvet chairs, holding his own counsel. It wouldn't do Raoul any harm to worry about Natasha. He himself wasn't concerned; he was certain that she had gone somewhere to seek some peace and regroup.

'I must find her,' Raoul said at last. 'I can't go on like this, not knowing where she is.'

'But why are you so anxious about a woman for whom you don't have deeper feelings?' Gaston murmured, tongue in cheek.

Raoul stopped in front of him eyes narrowed. 'You know damn well I love her, *mon ami*. It has been hard for me to admit, hard for me to realize, but the truth is I do, and I can't live without her.'

'Then the matter appears quite simple to me.'

'It does?' Raoul's brow flew up and he looked at his friend, bewildered.

'Tell her.' Gaston raised his hands in an expressive gesture. 'Tell her you love her.'

'How can I tell her if I don't know where the heck she is?' he replied, frustrated.

'I have a funny feeling that if you go over to the Manoir you might find her there. She may have needed a few hours to get her thoughts in line, her ducks in a row. But I don't think Natasha is one to run from adversity.'

'You think she's back?' Raoul's eyes narrowed. 'But what if she doesn't want me even when I tell her that—?' He cut off, stared out of the window, floored by the novelty of the situation. He had always been so sure of himself, in the driving seat, certain of the outcome. Now, suddenly, the tables had turned. And he hadn't a clue what might happen.

'The risk of having your pride trampled is one I'm afraid you'll have to take, *très cher*. Nothing really worthwhile in life is ever conquered easily. And sometimes there is a price to pay for our blindness.'

'Oh, stop all your damn moralizing,' Raoul snapped. 'If you really think she might be back then I should get over there and see that she's all right.'

With that he flung on his shooting jacket and swung out of the castle, determined to find out if his friend was right.

She heard the wheels crunching the gravel, knew instinctively that it was Raoul, and braced herself for a row.

When Henri showed him into the *grand salon*—the formality of which she had so deplored a help now in her moment of need—Natasha straightened her shoulders and prepared to face the music.

'Natasha,' he said, stopping as Henri closed the door discreetly behind him. 'Where have you been?' he demanded.

Natasha took a deep breath, determined to remain calm despite her racing pulse and thumping heart. 'It is not important, Raoul.'

'No,' he said suddenly, looking her over, filling his eyes with her, too relieved to see her safe. 'It isn't. What matters is that you have returned to me.'

'Raoul, I have not returned to you,' she said quietly, holding on to the small Louis Quinze table to her right for support. 'I came back to my home, that's all.'

He took several quick steps across the room and was standing over her before she could retreat. 'Natasha, I have been a fool and an idiot, and Gaston has spent the better part of the day telling me so.' He gave a quirky smile, very different from any she had seen before. 'Natasha, *mon amour*, I have come to tell you that I am that very fool that Gaston calls me. I am a fool because I saw things through the wrong pair of glasses. I saw them through the lenses of pride and honour and all those things that I have surrounded myself with all my life. I don't know if you will want me any more after the way I have behaved, so idiotically, but before you make any decision I need you to know one thing.' He stopped, gazed down at her, then reached for her left hand and raised it to his lips.

'Wh-what's that?' she whispered hoarsely.

'I love you. *Je t'aime, mon amour.* More than anything or anybody in the world. I never dreamed or thought that I could love like this, that I could feel such intense wonderful feelings for any woman. But you, *ma* Natasha, you have taught me differently. I swear that if you accept to marry me I will be a faithful loving husband to you till the day I die. I want you in every sense—in my arms, in my heart, in my life.'

Natasha felt her fingers tremble in his. She could hardly believe the words tumbling so sincerely from his lips.

'Raoul, I—'

'Tell me you love me too,' he said urgently, pulling her close. 'Tell me that all we have experienced together was as special and wonderful for you as it was for me, that you could never feel the same in the arms of any other man.' His eyes filled with a proprietary gleam.

A small smile escaped her. 'Oh, Raoul, my darling, you'll never change, will you?' she said, a tiny tender smile illuminating her face as her fingers touched his cheek and she read the anxiety and hope in his expression.

'My darling, I have changed. You have changed me. I don't guarantee that I will be— what is it you say in English?—a hen-pecked husband,' he said, his smile tender, 'but I will try and make you happy.'

'God forbid! A hen-pecked husband indeed.' Natasha burst out laughing as he hugged her tight. Then, drawing her against him, Raoul kissed her long and tenderly with a new, deep passion that obliterated any doubt she might still harbour as to his sincerity.

Then, drawing back, Raoul fished something out of his trouser pocket. 'I almost forgot,' he said, opening an ancient velvet pouch.

Natasha looked down, amazed, at the sparkling object lying in his palm, and when he took her left hand in his she swallowed.

'With this ring you become *ma promise*, my promised wife,' he said firmly, his eyes never leaving hers.

'It's beautiful,' she whispered, gazing from him to the ring and back.

'It is the ring Regis had made in Paris before the Revolution, when he planned to marry Natasha. It has been waiting in the vault all this time. Just for you.'

There was nothing left to say, nothing more to do but rest her head lovingly against his shoulder and feel the wondrous strength of his arms around her.

And as she did so a shadow on the terrace caught her eye. 'Look,' she murmured.

Raoul followed her gaze and together they held their breath. For out there, moving in the distance, were the old-fashioned shadowy figures of a man and a woman, disappearing hand in hand into the autumnal mist.

'We have come full circle,' Raoul whispered, when the moment had passed and all that remained were the leaves on the lawn. 'History has been righted. What a good thing I realized in time,' he muttered, with something of his old self-assurance.

With a shake of her head and a laugh, Natasha looked up at him, her eyes filled with love and mirth. 'Promise me you'll never change, Raoul.'

'But I just told you—' he protested.

'Shush,' she answered, placing her finger over his lips. 'I love you just the way you are.'

MILLS & BOON® PUBLISH EIGHT LARGE PRINT TITLES A MONTH. THESE ARE THE EIGHT TITLES FOR JANUARY 2006

———————— ❦ ————————

THE RAMIREZ BRIDE
Emma Darcy

EXPOSED: THE SHEIKH'S MISTRESS
Sharon Kendrick

THE SICILIAN MARRIAGE
Sandra Marton

AT THE FRENCH BARON'S BIDDING
Fiona Hood-Stewart

THEIR NEW-FOUND FAMILY
Rebecca Winters

THE BILLIONAIRE'S BRIDE
Jackie Braun

CONTRACTED: CORPORATE WIFE
Jessica Hart

IMPOSSIBLY PREGNANT
Nicola Marsh

MILLS & BOON®

Live the emotion

1205 R